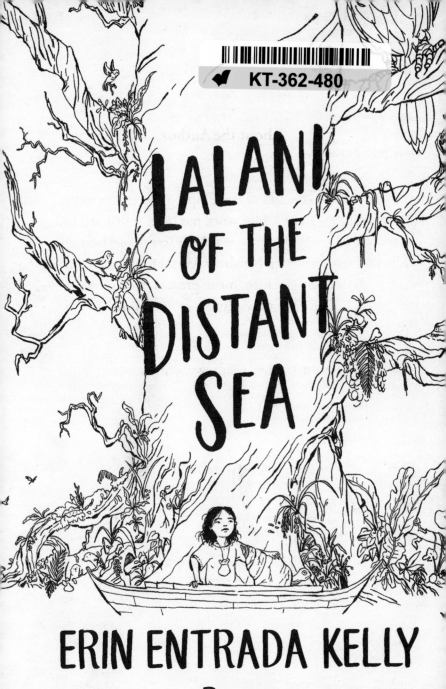

LALANI OF THE DISTANT SEA

ERIN ENTRADA KELLY

Piccadilly
PRESS

This edition published 2020 by Picadilly Press

First published in Great Britain in 2019 by
PICCADILLY PRESS
80–81 Wimpole St, London W1G 9RE
www.piccadillypress.co.uk

Text copyright © Erin Entrada Kelly, 2019
Illustrations and map copyright © Lian Cho, 2019

A CIP catalogue record for this book is available from the British Library.

ISBN: 978-1-84812-915-3
also available as an ebook

1

Printed and bound by Clays Ltd, Elcograf S.p.A.

MIX
Paper from
responsible sources
FSC® C018072

Piccadilly Press is an imprint of Bonnier Books UK
www.bonnierbooks.co.uk

LALANI
OF THE
DISTANT
SEA

About the Author

ERIN ENTRADA KELLY is a Filipino-American writer of children's books. Her work has been translated into several languages and she is a *New York Times* bestseller. She received the 2018 Newbery Medal for *Hello, Universe*. Netflix is currently in the process of adapting *Hello, Universe* into a feature film.

For more information, visit www.erinentradakelly.com

LALANI
OF THE
DISTANT
SEA

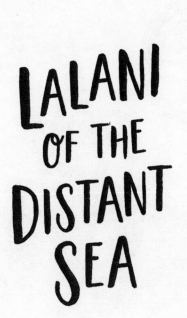

Mount
Kahna

Menyoro

Loomers

Village

Isa

Whenbo Forest

Bai Vinca

Goyuk Hive

Veiled Sea

Shipbuilders

Northern Shore

School

Sanlagita

There are stories of extraordinary children who are chosen from birth to complete great quests and conquer evil villains.

This is no such story.

Sometimes, you are an ordinary child.

Sometimes, you choose yourself.

Come closer. Nestle deep. Travel now to two mountains. They are alive, at least to those who live among them. One of them towers darkly. It casts a shadow of vengeance, impatience, and fear. The Sanlagitans call it Mount Kahna.

The other mountain—if you can call it that—is bathed in light. Set foot here, and you will have all of life's good fortunes, whatever those may be. This is Mount Isa.

You can't see Isa now. No human has ever laid eyes on her. Nevertheless, the Sanlagitans are certain the mountain calls to them. They die trying to answer. They attempt journey after journey. They are pushed by their faith, not knowing that they believe in the wrong things.

Their ships sink. Their hearts break. And yet, they make the trip, because they feel Isa's presence on an invisible horizon. Somewhere far away, yet close enough to touch. Somewhere beyond the distant sea.

The Three of Them

Twelve-year-old Lalani Sarita had heard the story of the mountain beast many times. She knew of his mangled face, his house of stolen treasures, and his penchant for evil trickery, but she begged to hear it all again anyway. It was the perfect night for ghost stories. The moon cast a bluish glow through the slats of the Yuzi house, and jars of bulb flies shined like stars in the corners of the front room. Lo Yuzi leaned forward in her rocking chair to eye the members of her audience closely. There were three of them, of course: Lalani; her best friend, Veyda; and Veyda's younger brother, Hetsbi.

"Imagine you are an old man," Lo Yuzi, who was Veyda and Hetsbi's mother, said. She spoke in the loudest of whispers, and the chair creaked when she moved. Her hands, rough and scarred from years of pulling plants, sat folded on her lap. "Your face is weary with wrinkles, and your nose is missing."

Lalani pressed her palms to her cheeks and pulled them down, imagining her face sagging with age. Hetsbi, who was only one year younger than the girls, laughed behind a closed fist.

"You live on Mount Kahna," Lo Yuzi continued. "You spend your days all alone, dreaming of your other life, when you had friends and family. But you know that this life is what you're due, because of all your sins. And one day, a brave but frightened boy decides to climb the mountain, even though all the villagers tell him not to." Her expression darkened. "'Mount Kahna doesn't wish to be disturbed!' the villagers say. 'It will eat you alive!'" She snatched at the air in front of their faces and they all flinched, even though she'd done this dozens of times before. "And you know they're right, because the mountain only loves evil things, like you. But this boy doesn't listen to the villagers. He fills his lucky bronze canteen and sets out anyway. And this makes you happy because—"

"Wait," said Hetsbi, frowning. "You forgot the eyes."

Oh, right! Lalani realized that, too. The eyes were the most important part of the story.

Veyda tossed her long, raven hair over her shoulder and braided it, something she did when she was impatient.

"Ah, yes, the eyes," Lo Yuzi said. She sighed and leaned back. *Creak.* "I suppose we'll have to start again another time."

"Just backtrack a little bit and we can keep going," said Lalani quickly.

"I'd rather start a new path than trace old ones," Lo Yuzi said. "Besides, it's time for sleep. We need to wake as early as we can to beat the sun."

But there was no point in that, and they all knew it. There'd been no rain for months, and the heat was relentless. It didn't matter what time you woke up, you were going to sweat.

Veyda was already half standing. Lo Yuzi snapped her fingers toward her daughter and motioned for her to sit back down. "We have benediction."

Veyda sighed and took her seat again.

Lo Yuzi bowed her head. Lalani did, too.

"Mount Kahna," they all said in unison—although Lalani suspected Veyda wasn't saying a word. "Spare us another night. Remain quiet and peaceful in our gratitude."

Once they were nestled in their oostrum-stuffed blankets, which splayed across the floor of the sleeping room, Veyda grumbled as usual about the benedictions.

"It's so silly," she whispered. She turned on her side to face Lalani. Lo Yuzi was in the basin room, rinsing the vegetables they'd picked earlier that day. "Why are we asking a mountain to remain quiet? Mountains are mountains."

"Don't say that!" said Hetsbi. Lalani didn't know another boy who spooked as easily as Hetsbi. Maybe because he didn't have a father to show him all the ways of men. Then again, many boys didn't. Not if they were children of sailors, as the three of them were.

The life of a sailor didn't last long in Sanlagita, after all.

"Either way, it's a good story," Lalani said. "I wish my mother told stories like that."

She thought of her mother's lined face and tired eyes.

"But that's all it is. A *story*. This place has too many of those," said Veyda.

"Maybe you should go climb it then," Hetsbi said, elbowing her in the back. "Since it's 'just a mountain.' Take a canteen and go up tomorrow and let's see how brave you are."

"I have more important things to do," said Veyda. "I need plants for Toppi's salve."

Toppi Oragleo, the sick baby three houses down.

Lalani pushed her blanket away with her feet. Too

warm for a blanket. Too warm for anything.

"I'll help you pick them," Lalani said.

Veyda smiled mournfully. "I'm not sure I'll need much help, sola. There aren't many plants left."

"Speaking of Toppi," Hetsbi said excitedly. "His sisters said they found hair on the rocks along the southern shore. *Ziva's* hair."

"Really?" Lalani said. Veyda rolled her eyes. "How do they know it's Ziva's?"

"It was long and black and stretched between the rocks like a web!" Hetsbi said, weaving his narrow fingers together. "There's no other explanation."

"All the women in the village have long, black hair," Veyda said. "It could belong to anyone."

Hetsbi dropped his arms to his sides. "But how did it get between the rocks then?"

"Any number of ways," said Veyda. "Like I said, this place has too many stories. We need to solve real problems, like how I'm going to make medicine without any plants."

The three of them lay there, silently.

That was a real problem indeed.

"Maybe we can ask the mountain for rain," Lalani said softly.

"I'm not asking the mountain for anything," Hetsbi whispered. "What if the mountain beast hears us? What if he's listening now, with his pointed ears, and he comes and steals us in our sleep?"

"They're just stories," Veyda said.

Lalani took her friend's hand and squeezed. "I'll ask, just in case."

She closed her eyes. *Please, Kahna, give us rain.* Her imagination floated up and up the mountain, trying to picture a peaceful benefactor. Instead, she saw the beast, just as Lo Yuzi described—except now he had sharp, pointed claws. He scrambled toward her, scuttering like a tree creature, toppling treasures in his wake.

Give me your eyes, he hissed. *And you can have anything you wish for.*

House of Light

When Lalani woke up the next morning, the sun had not yet risen over the island of Sanlagita. She found Veyda sitting on the floor of the front room with an empty basket.

"Look at these plants," said Veyda. There were a few leaves in the basket's cradle, but nothing compared to the usual number. She lifted one. Brown and wilted. "I don't know if I can use this for anything, and the baby's cough is only getting worse."

Toppi. A wiggly little boy with three older sisters. The girls had names, of course, but since they were rarely seen apart they were known simply as the Oragleo sisters. And their brother, the first boy of the family, had been sick for days. Their mother was so desperate that she had asked for Veyda's help. In secrecy—no one could ever know that a twelve-year-old girl was dispensing medicine. Not even Toppi's father, Maddux, and he was a good man. But in Sanlagita, girls had to keep secrets. Especially from the village menyoro, the man who watched over them all.

"Is there anything we can do?" Lalani asked, squatting next to her.

Veyda dropped the leaf and shrugged. "We need rain. It has to come eventually, right?"

Lalani was quiet.

"You should get home soon," said Veyda, standing. "There are men already on the water."

Lalani stood, too. Reluctantly. She hated going home. Veyda's house was alive with stories and big imaginations. And although Lalani's house looked the same, as did all the houses in the village—built with wooden slats from felled trees; front, sleeping, and basin rooms for daily living—the atmosphere was something else altogether. There were invisible shadows in Lalani's house and a charged air.

There were no shadows in the Yuzi house.

Only light.

Girl on the Rocks

Ziva could have been saved by her hair. Instead, it was hacked off and she slipped into the Veiled Sea, never to be seen again.

Veyda was right about Sanlagita and its stories. And of those tales, the story of Ziva was Lalani's favorite.

Mora Pasa, an old woman with deep valleys of wrinkles, was the only person left on the island who had known Ziva—not as a ghost, but as a living, breathing girl. Mora was an elderly matriarch of a spiteful family of loomers that Lalani often visited to get thread for her mother. Every time she did, she asked Mora to tell her about Ziva.

Mora told it the same way every time:

"She was smart, like your friend Veyda," Mora would say. "But she was cursed. It was clear from the moment she was born. She looked like no other infant in the village. Her smooth brown skin was tainted with stains of deep red, like blood that could not be washed away. The birthmark stretched from her neck to her ears, as if it was alive and crawling up her face. There was nothing the menyoro could do. He warned all of us—even the little children, like I was at the time—to avoid Ziva or risk being cursed ourselves. Her parents were ashamed. Ziva was made to feel ashamed, too. Her life was weighted with misery. She escaped in the stories of Sanlagita. Especially the story of Mount Isa. She believed, with all her heart, that there was an island to the north that held all of life's good fortunes. But the menyoro would never make her a sailor. A girl sailor! And a cursed one at that! Can you imagine?"

No, Lalani could not.

According to Mora Pasa, Ziva was only thirteen years

old when she hid on a ship on Sailing Day. Ziva believed that the men could not—would not—turn her away once they were out to sea. Not a young girl like her.

Oh, how wrong she was.

Mora Pasa insisted that Ziva had been kind when she was alive. But death had made her angry and vengeful. According to the villagers, she stalked the island's shores. When she was in a particularly foul mood, she dragged the fish so far down that no hook could reach them. Once a village fisherman was caught in a sudden storm and drowned, and that was blamed on Ziva, too.

Some even blamed her for the lack of rain.

But Lalani knew better.

"I know it's not you who dried the earth," Lalani whispered to Ziva now as she veered off the central path and walked briskly to the southern shore. "And I know it's not your fault for being born with a mark."

If I had known you then, Lalani thought, *we would have been friends.*

In the very early morning, the shore was covered with

fishing boats for as far as the eye could see. But many of the fishermen were already on the water now, so only a few remained—a daring few, considering that the menyoro sometimes made surprise inspections to find out who was lazy and sleeping in.

Then again, children weren't supposed to dally, either. Today Lalani decided she would check the rock bed quickly, then she'd go straight home. Who knows? Maybe the Oragleo sisters had missed something in plain view.

The sounds of fishermen calling to one another swelled with the sun. The absence of clouds made it feel like midafternoon. Sweat trickled between Lalani's shoulder blades as she navigated the rocks. The rock bed could be dangerous—one slip could easily snap a bone. Luckily the rocks were mostly dry. The tide hadn't come up this far lately.

"Ziva," Lalani said quietly as she balanced herself. "If I find your hair, I promise I will only show Veyda and Hetsbi. We will keep it a secret."

Although Lalani was one of many Sanlagitans who had searched these rocks for signs of Ziva, she felt that she did it with greater purpose. She was more interested in the girl than the ghost. The one who was punished for sins she didn't commit. The one with dreams of escape. Lalani tried to imagine herself hiding on a ship, crouching in a dark corner, desperate to find something better. But that was something she could never do. How brave Ziva must have been, even if it hadn't ended well for anyone.

"I know you didn't mean any harm," Lalani said. "If I find your hair, I will cherish it forever."

She'd searched this shoal many times before, but it had never appeared so vast. Half the bed was typically underwater. She relied on her well-practiced routine: balance on two sturdy rocks, then squat and look for strands of hair. Move to the next pair of rocks, repeat.

Every now and then she'd find old fishing wire or an old piece of netting, and she'd carry them home for her mother. But today, the rocks offered little.

She moved farther and farther out, both arms raised

for balance. The rocks became flatter and smoother. At first Lalani thought this would help her, but there was a downside to these friendly surfaces: they had no grip, and neither did her sandals. When her foot slipped the first time, the unexpected glide startled her, and she felt unbalanced even when she managed to stand straight up. Her heart raced.

The water lapped more loudly here.

How far out had she'd come, anyway?

She turned.

The shore was farther away than she expected, but it wasn't an impossible distance. All she had to do was backtrack, rock by rock.

How long had she been exploring?

All the fishing boats but one were out to sea now. She saw the pitched roofs of the village. It was time to get home.

She stepped carefully.

When had the rocks become so slippery?

She tried to step in the same places—after all, if she'd

made it across before, surely she would again—but she couldn't remember exactly which ones she'd stepped on.

Her foot slipped again. She waved her arms to regain her balance and did.

The sound of the water surged in her ears.

She didn't like water.

Yes, she lived on an island.

Yes, it always surrounded her.

But she didn't like it. She wasn't afraid of the water itself. It was being *inside* the water that terrified her. She wasn't a swimmer. Not many on the island were. Why would they need to be? Only the sailors and fishermen were ever on the water, and there were many fishermen who didn't know how to swim, either. The sailors were the strongest swimmers—the strongest at everything, really—so they were the ones who could best find their way back home using only their arms and legs.

Theoretically.

Lalani and Veyda had talked about the idea of swimming many times. When pieces of broken ships drifted back to shore, they'd wonder: Could the men have survived? Did they swim? Did our fathers swim somewhere? Are they still alive?

I don't think it's hard to swim, do you? Veyda would say. *You kick your legs, sweep your arms in front of you, and move through the water like a fish. Right?*

What did Lalani know of swimming?

The water was shallow here, at least. But still—

She took a step. And another.

She was still on the smooth rocks. A few more steps, and she'd have more grip.

She'd just become sure of herself when her sandal hit a small wet patch, smaller than a pebble, and *bam*! She went down. She hit the rock with her knee. A line of fire shot up her leg. She hadn't fallen in the water, but who cared about that blessing? The pain was so great she screamed. She leaned forward, palms splayed on the rocks in front of her. She shifted back and sat on the wet rock. She studied her leg. A thick clot of blood oozed from the wound.

"Ugh," she groaned.

She eyed the shore, wondering how she would get there with a banged and bloody knee. What if she fell again? She studied the fishing boats, no more than dots bobbing on the horizon now. Her knee throbbed. She wished she knew which boat belonged to her uncle, so she could make a silent request to Mount Kahna. *Kahna, if you can hear me, please pull Drum underwater.*

"Lalani!" A man called her name. Maddux Oragleo, Toppi's father. He was walking along the shore, headed to his fishing boat. "Do you need help?"

Before she could say no, he was on his way to her, skillfully stepping across the rocks. He pulled her to her feet and frowned at the blood on her knee.

"You'll need to wrap that tight," he said. "I can fetch the menyoro if you'd like. Perhaps he can help you with the injury?"

"Oh, there's no need," Lalani replied. "I'm sorry to inconvenience you."

They walked back to the shore together. Something—a wallecta—scampered by. They sidestepped it, with Lalani holding tight to the crook of Maddux's arm. Wallecta were small creatures who often played near the water. They were sweet, but cautious. Lalani and Veyda had tried to tame one once. But wallecta weren't meant to be tamed.

Drum often told Lalani she was as useless as a wallecta. *But at least wallecta have small bites of meat to offer us*, he'd say. *What do you have?*

"I'm sorry Toppi's sick," Lalani said. She wasn't sure if it was the right thing to say, but she meant it. How unfair it was, she thought, for Toppi to suffer when he'd done nothing wrong.

But then, any suffering was terrible—wasn't it?

"Thank you, Lalani," Maddux said.

Lalani let go of Maddux's arm, relieved to be on solid ground again.

"There's so much heartache for everyone these days, as we wait for the rain," Maddux continued. "It's kind of you to think of our Toppi."

"I wish I could do more for him," Lalani said. "Me and Veyda, too."

"You're kind girls. You do what you can," Maddux replied. "And that's what matters."

As Maddux walked away, Lalani felt a stitch of guilt in her gut. He'd said—twice—that she was kind. But she'd wished harm on her uncle moments ago.

If Maddux knew, would he still think she was a kind girl?

Probably not, she thought.

House of Shadows

Drum, Lalani's uncle, cast the darkest shadow in the house. Lalani's real father had died, together with Veyda's, years before. He had been a Sanlagitan sailor, which meant his life was celebrated and short. Very few men were selected by the menyoro to sail for Isa, where all of life's good fortunes were said to be, and these men were the strongest, cleverest, or most skilled. The men most likely to survive.

But they never did.

Her father's death had left Lalani and her mother, one of the village menders, alone. But not for long.

Lalani's uncle came knocking on their door soon enough. He'd lost his wife to mender's disease and had a son, Kul, who needed looking after. Lalani and her mother wanted nothing to do with them. Drum's temper was legendary, and his son was no better. They were dangerous and sturdy, the pair of them. But how could Lalani's mother say no to her dead husband's older brother? It was a match that made perfect sense, at least to the menyoro and Drum.

Lalani had been eight years old, and she remembered the day vividly. The sky was clear, but a storm had entered their house. Suddenly she had a second father who towered over her, and a scowling brother who was four years older and built like cleaved rock.

The men took up a lot of space. Not just in the sleeping room, where Lalani and her mother nestled in a corner, but in other ways, too.

They were fishermen. The smell of sweat, scales, and water crept into every part of the house.

They were big. Their footfalls shook the floor.

And they were loud. Lalani knew them by the sound of their boots hitting the ground. The door slamming shut. Demands being made. *Mend this shirt. Wash this fruit. Gut the fish.*

And she knew them by their tells. That's what she called the little hints that told her what was going on in someone's head. When Veyda braided her hair, it meant she was impatient. When Lo Yuzi lifted her shoulders, it meant her story was almost over. And when her uncle drummed his fingers against his leg, it meant he was angry. And when he was angry, he was frightening.

So that's how Lalani thought of him: Drum. He had a name, of course. But his shadow was so dark that Lalani rarely thought of it.

Drum and Kul weren't there when Lalani finally made it home. They often left before light to get the best catch. Her mother was awake, sitting in the front room, surrounded by baskets of village clothing and swaths of fabric. Her head was bent over her work.

Sometimes she became so focused that she barely knew what was happening around her.

"Good morning, Mama," Lalani said.

Lalani had limped through the village, but she'd had the sense to wipe the weeping lines of blood away with the hem of her dress. Now that she was home, she picked up the first scrap of discarded fabric she saw, sat in the chair next to her mother, and tied the stiff material around her knee. Her mother didn't ask any questions.

The room was dimly lit—the sun still in the east—but her mother could mend no matter what. She was good at her job, which meant the menyoro assigned her more clothes and fishing nets than the other menders. Never mind that mending was already one of the most dangerous tasks in Sanlagita.

Truth be told, Lalani didn't enjoy sitting next to her mother while she was mending. It made her heart catch to see her mother's skin near the needle.

"See how I thread these close together?" her mother said, lifting a shirt to Lalani's eyes. "If you space your stitches too far apart, your seam will have a hole. No good."

Lalani nodded.

"But you don't want them too close together, either," her mother added, going back to work. Her dark hair fell around her face. "Wastes thread. And then the loomers complain to the menyoro."

Lalani nodded again. The needle moved swiftly in, out, the point barely a breath from her mother's fingers. So many menders died in Sanlagita, which made it an unenviable job. Even Lo Yuzi was grateful to spend her days in the blazing sun, harvesting food, rather than sitting indoors with a stack of mending and the threat of mender's disease.

"I thought you were mending nets today," Lalani said. "I saw a pile near the door."

"I'll wait until sunset. Too hot to sit outside," her mother said. "If the rain doesn't come, I may have to bring the nets in."

Lalani scrunched up her nose, thinking of all the

smelly fish guts and scales that would trail inside the house behind the damaged nets.

Once the seam was complete, her mother neatly folded the shirt, laid it in the basket at her right foot, and reached for the next item.

"Mama?" Lalani said, after several moments of silence.

"Hm?"

"Do you know any stories?

"Stories?"

"Yes. Maybe stories from your childhood or something. Like the story of the beast who lives in Mount Kahna."

Her mother tightened her mouth, then lowered her voice and said, "Don't speak of the mountain outside of benediction. The menyoro says all we have to fear is the wrath of Mount Kahna."

Lalani paused, frowning. "Do you know any, though?"

Her mother's hands stilled. She gazed off at something in the distance—a memory, perhaps.

"My mother used to tell me a story," she said.

Lalani sat up straighter. "Really?"

"She said it was a story she heard from *her* mother. And the mother before her."

Lalani had never known any mothers in her family but her own. She imagined them now, a long line of weary women, telling tales to one another.

"How did the story go?" Lalani asked.

"All I recall is the first line."

"What was the first line?"

"'Imagine a place where the binty sing.'"

A place where the binty sing? Lalani had never heard of such a thing. The binty were small and useless birds. A curious creature to build a tale around. And everyone knew birds didn't sing. A singing bird— what a funny thought.

Lalani's mind swam with anticipation.

But her mother was not Lo Yuzi. She bowed her head, back to her mending.

"I don't remember the rest," she mumbled. "Best to focus on work."

YOU ARE WHERE
THE BINTY SING

Imagine a place where the binty sing. An island far in the north, where they raise their heads like majestic gods and bring forth the most beautiful birdsong you've ever heard. You don't think birds can sing, do you? It sounds foolish, I know. They don't sing in Sanlagita, that's true. They are quiet here and sullen and feathered with ash. They have lost their voices. Or perhaps they never knew they

had voices. Is that the same thing?

In the north, they have lost nothing. In the north, on Mount Isa, the binty are beautiful. I don't know what makes them sing, and I have never heard it. So, I imagine.

When I have impossible questions, I answer by imagining.

In my mind, birdsong sounds like the sweetest drip of nectar.

It sounds like the shining sun of all the island's daughters.

It sounds like light in the darkness. A rising moon.

It sounds like calm after a peaceful sleep, just before you open your eyes.

Don't be frightened. Why would something like this frighten you, my little daughter?

Shh. Shh.

Listen.

What does the binty sound like to you?

Pardon Me

Boom. Boom. The sound of Drum's boots hitting the floor. *Thunk, thunk:* now Kul's. They strode in, smelling of fish and water, as Lalani gathered a basket of mended clothes. They were home early. But it was clear from the looks on their faces that things had not gone well. Again.

"The fish aren't biting," Drum grumbled. He filled a cup from the basin and drank deeply. Water dripped down his chin. When he was finished, he stepped aside and leaned against the wall near the door. Kul drank and did the same. "And why are there so many nets waiting to be mended?" Drum asked.

"It's too hot to sit outside," Lalani's mother replied.

"My son and I were outside all day, and we survived. You can't manage to mend a few nets?" Drum snorted and shook his head. "Useless, you are."

"Useless," Kul repeated. "The menyoro may have to cut rations if the rain doesn't come. If you don't do your work, we'll be the first to lose our share."

"She's doing her work," Lalani said, pointing to the basket of mended clothes.

Kul narrowed his eyes at her. "No one asked you, sahyoon. And what's wrong with your knee?"

"I fell."

"Idiot," Kul said.

Drum took another drink of water, then said, "We've never had a dry season like this."

"The menyoro should go from house to house and demand more benedictions," Kul said. "This is punishment from Kahna. Or trickery by that marked ghost woman."

"Her name is Ziva," Lalani said.

"Who cares what her name is?" Kul snapped.

Drum strode toward Lalani's mother, who gathered the clothes from her lap as his shadow fell over her. She soundlessly surrendered her chair. He sat down as she placed her work on the table and kept mending.

"You best keep an eye out," Drum said to her. He leaned back in the chair. "If you get sick, you'll be no use."

She nodded without looking up, then lifted her chin to the basket of mended clothes. "Bring those to the loomers, Lalani," she said. "And ask for the next bundle of rations. I'm nearly out of thread."

Lalani was more than happy to go. The day was still hot, dry, and brutal, but it was better than being inside with the shadows. She pulled the basket into the crook of her arm and headed toward the door. Kul blocked her way. He glared down at her and grinned. An evil grin. He was good at those.

"Pardon me," Lalani said.

"Pardon *me*," he replied. There was a sneer in his voice. There always was.

He shifted aside, just enough for her to leave. And she did—quickly—even though it pained her to walk that fast.

The Loomers

Menders died on the island of Sanlagita. More than you would expect. The exact cause of the disease was a mystery, but many Sanlagitans believed it was punishment for poor or sloppy work.

Here was what the villagers knew for certain: mender's disease struck after a pricked finger, but not every pricked finger made menders sick. If you were lucky, you'd spill some blood and that would be it. But if you were unlucky . . . well, you faced a short and tragic future.

The first symptom was fever, usually within twenty-four hours. You'd notice a warmth in your chest. A rosiness in your cheeks. Sweat along your hairline. Not long after that, the secret thoughts buried in the corner of your mind crept into the light, and you'd find yourself making confessions—ones you never intended to make. Lalani and Veyda had once visited a sick elderly mender. Veyda had medicine that she thought would help. It lowered the woman's temperature, but did nothing to ease the fever in her mind. While Veyda was rubbing ointment on her temples, the old woman had motioned them closer.

"When my sister fell sick, she would send me to pick up her rations. She was so weak, she could hardly move," the old woman whispered. Her breath was stale, and her lips cracked. "I stole from her every time. Kahna, forgive me."

After the confessions came the swelling. Your cheeks and throat swelled like a yoonfish. That's when you knew for certain that you'd soon be dead, often within ten days.

According to legend, there was a singular cure for mender's disease nestled inside the petals of a miraculous flower. The flower was bright yellow, speckled with flecks of white, but it only grew on Mount Isa—one of many good fortunes that existed on the northern island.

Was it true? Veyda said it was just another tall tale. But no one knew for sure, because the sailors who journeyed across the water never returned. Only pieces of their ships did.

Lalani thought about this as she made her way through the village with the basket bumping against her skinny, brown leg. Another sailing day was coming up soon. Three sailors would set off into the sea this time, and the entire village would gather at the shore to bid them farewell.

Lalani didn't look forward to it.

It made her think of her father. And Veyda's. And how they, too, had set off with big dreams. How the villagers had waved and cheered. Lalani had been little then, but she still remembered the way the ship had disappeared into the mist, never to be seen again.

But no use to mull over bad memories. She had just walked past the line of tubs where the washers worked. The women lifted their eyes and smiled at her. Some had small girls with them who wanted nothing more than to splash in the water that was meant for the clothes. Who could blame them? It was so hot. Lalani waved, even though the women couldn't wave back because their arms were plunged deep into the water, scrubbing, scrubbing, scrubbing dirty clothes, many of which would eventually find their way to one of the menders. Two of the washers were old and tired, their backs perpetually rounded from decades of bending over the basins.

Lalani squinted as the sunlight moved across the path. There wasn't a cloud in the sky.

Kahna towered in the distance. The loomers lived along the foot of the mountain because it was an ideal place to raise shek. Lalani saw them now, round and heavy with soft, white fur that would be sheared and spun into thread. Many of them had been sheared already.

Bosalene Pasa stood in the doorway of her house, which also served as a work hut for the loomers, with her hands on her hips. Her mouth was a straight, tight line, and she wielded judgment like a weapon. Her sons Bio and Dah were the same way. Luckily, the boys in

Sanlagita went to school during the day, so they were rarely there when Lalani picked up her mother's thread.

Veyda could hardly stomach the idea of boys like Bio and Dah learning new trades and skills when she and Lalani could not. *No amount of schooling could give them brains*, Veyda often said.

"Are those my clothes?" Bosalene asked. A wide fence encircled her small plot of land—a pen for the shek. Only it didn't look like they had much to graze on. The land had turned brown.

"How are the shek?" Lalani asked as she handed the basket to Bosalene and craned her neck to find her favorite. She had secretly named him My-Shek, because she thought of him as hers. She was the one who had first noticed the black patch behind his ear, after all.

Bosalene sorted through the basket, then balanced it on her hip.

"Not good," she said. "We need rain. What's wrong with your leg?"

"I fell," Lalani replied absently. "Is Mora Pasa home?"

Lalani wanted to ask Mora Pasa if she knew the story of the binty, so she could tell it to her mother. What a wonderful gift it would be, Lalani thought, to tell her mother a tale that she'd long forgotten.

"My mother is asleep. She's not feeling well, you know," Bosalene said. "Probably because of girls like you running around her all the time, asking for old legends."

Lalani turned her attention to the shek again to hide her disappointment. The animals were clustered near the fence. Probably looking for any greenery they could find. The mountain slope looked plush with grass, but no one dared to set an animal or person free on the mountain. Who knew what Kahna would do?

"I don't have your mother's thread rations just yet," Bosalene said. "But I will tomorrow."

Lalani promised to return the next day, then headed back the way she'd come. She walked slowly and tried to distract herself from the pain in her knee by whispering some of Lo Yuzi's stories to the air. But before long she could think of nothing but the fire in her leg and the dryness of the earth.

Valiant Hetsbi

There was only one way to know which boys in Sanlagita were meant to be sailors, shipbuilders, or fishermen: you had to put them to the task.

Unfortunately, Hetsbi Yuzi was horrendous at everything.

For shipbuilding instruction, the youngest boys—ages six and seven—first learned how to identify and fell superior trees. Once they reached age eleven, they were supposed to have the skills to build a small fishing boat, big enough for two.

Hetsbi had started his project with the best of

intentions. He planned to build a mighty boat, one that any Sanlagita fisherman could take into the water. A boat that could carry a thousand nets, if needed. How hard could it be? He could be successful if he followed the instructions and watched the stronger boys, like Cade Malay.

Or so he thought.

Then he started building and discovered that his hands wouldn't do what he wanted them to. He wanted to sand the timber smooth, but his hands moved sloppily. He wanted to hammer the nails straight, but his hands missed their marks. He wanted to build a boat that would make jaws drop. *We were wrong*, the villagers would mutter. *We were wrong about Hetsbi.*

But they weren't.

His boat was a failure.

And everyone was about to find out.

The boys stood in a line near the northern shore, a mile trek from the schoolyard, facing their instructor, Taiting. The Veiled Sea roiled under its strange fog behind them. All ten boys were focused on Taiting. Each of them held his boat upright, ready for inspection.

Taiting was built like a meha cane—tall and lean, but hearty. He was kind, but firm. Despite his knotted knees, Taiting moved elegantly as he made his way down the line.

"Well done, Bio," he said to the Pasa boy. Hetsbi's heart thundered. "No doubt your father will be pleased for you to take this home."

That was the prize for building an operable boat— the boys were able to take their boats back with them to the village, so the fishermen could put them to use. The unusable boats were thrown in a pile of scraps with last year's failures.

Taiting moved on to Bio's brother, Dah Pasa.

"A bit more sanding here, Dah," Taiting said. "You don't want the men getting splinters in their feet."

"Yes, Taiting," said Dah.

Cade Malay's boat was next. Cade wore his ax-saw around his waist, like he was ready to fell a tree at any moment. The other boys carried the ax-saw in slings. The knives had short, serrated blades that curved at the end, and Hetsbi was always afraid his would nick his skin if he wore it too close. But Cade wasn't scared. He had a quality Hetsbi envied. An easy confidence. According to Taiting, his boat was in perfect condition. No surprise there.

"You're a skilled builder, like your brother," said Taiting. "There is much hope for Sailing Day."

Oh, yes. Hetsbi had been so preoccupied with his project that he'd forgotten about Sailing Day—Cade's brother and two cousins would be the first to sail in years. How could he have forgotten?

Cade did not respond.

"No doubt your hands show the marks of hard work," Taiting continued. He inspected Cade's hands—roughened, torn, with blisters where he'd held the tools—and nodded approvingly.

Hetsbi put his hands behind his back.

His were blistered, too.

His skin had turned to tree bark.

Every knuckle ached.

But what did he have to show for it?

"Aha," said Taiting, now standing in front of Hetsbi, with Hetsbi's boat between them. "Let's take a look."

Taiting leaned forward and craned his long neck this way and that, eyeing the belly of Hetsbi's pathetic vessel.

Hetsbi heard the Pasa boys snicker, as loud as thunder.

"I see a streak of auburn here," Taiting said.

The boats were meant to be smoothed clean. Unblemished. But on the last day of construction, the tender and overworked skin between Hetsbi's index finger and thumb finally broke, and drops of blood had plunked down on the boat, like fat teardrops. He'd sanded them into the wood. What choice did he have?

"An imperfection," said Hetsbi quietly.

What would Taiting make of a boy who'd worked so hard and done so little?

The instructor crouched and moved along the edge of the boat on his haunches, like an insect ready to pounce.

He had nearly reached Hetsbi's feet when he frowned.

"I'm afraid the nose of the vessel is too narrow and uneven," Taiting said.

"Yes," said Hetsbi.

A spattering of quiet laughter spread among the other boys. Hetsbi kept his eyes down.

"It will never navigate well in the water," Taiting said.

"I understand," said Hetsbi.

The teacher stood. He towered over Hetsbi.

"It was a valiant effort," he said.

Mouthful of Yoonfish

After the sun set and the family had their plates of fish, Lalani asked if she could stay at Veyda's house again.

Drum spoke before her mother could answer.

"You spend too much time with that girl," he said. A flake of fish sat on his lip. He drummed two large fingers against the table and eyed Lalani suspiciously. "There's something not right about the Yuzis. That girl's got ideas in her head. And the boy's so useless, he may as well be a girl. A boy who's afraid of his own feet will never become a man."

Kul chuckled through a mouthful of yoonfish.

Lalani twisted her hands in her lap. "She's my best friend," she said.

"What do you girls do over there, anyway?" Kul asked. "Talk about your lost papas?"

He chuckled again.

Lalani's mother lifted her eyes. They landed on Kul. Hard.

"You may go to Veyda's, Lalani," she said.

The only time her mother showed defiance was when someone spoke out against her first husband.

Your father was kind, but too strong for his own good, she used to say, back when she still mentioned him. *Kahna forgive me, but there were times I wished he were weak or ill. Then the menyoro would never have chosen him to sail.*

Only the bravest and strongest were selected as sailors. They were Sanlagita's best chance. The fact that her father had been a sailor and Drum was a fisherman—a class of workers lower than the shipbuilders—was a secret source of pride for both Lalani and her mother, even if they'd never admitted it out loud, even to each other.

Lalani thanked her mother and stood up before Drum could protest. She gathered her plate, placed it in the basin, and rushed out the door.

The walk to Veyda's house didn't take long, and it brought Lalani near the village pump, where she often helped herself to a handful of water. She saw Agapito Malay, one of Cade's older brothers, standing guard with his arms crossed.

"The water is being heavily rationed," Agapito said, not unkindly. "You can only take from the pump if you have a special bowl issued by the menyoro. Do you have a bowl?"

"No," Lalani said.

He sighed. "When it rains again, things will get better."

"I understand," said Lalani. She stepped away to continue her journey to Veyda's, then stopped and turned. "Your brother is sailing soon."

He shifted his eyes away.

"I'll be there to see him off, along with the rest of the village," she said. "I wish him the best."

Agapito nodded. He said nothing else.

YOU ARE SANLAGITAN

Imagine you're a Sanlagitan. Things are as they've always been. You don't know how your people arrived on this island. All you know is that you are here now.

Look at the pitched roofs of the flenka houses, covered with thick meha leaves. There is the water well, in the center of the village. And here is the schoolhouse, where boys learn to become men.

To the west is Mount Kahna—wide, dark, and looming. When you were little, the grown-ups told you stories of boys who went exploring there and were never seen again. No one dares to explore Kahna anymore—

it's believed the mountain is hungry and eats whatever passes. It may barrel down to the village and devour you all. So, in the morning and night, you whisper a simple benediction to spare your souls.

Something curious, though: men no longer explore Mount Kahna, but they continue sailing north, even though no one has returned from there, either. Perhaps because that legend is too hard to resist. Or perhaps because they discovered fortunes after all and chose not to return. But, no—that can't be it, because you know about all the terrible things that have happened. Ziva, the lock of her hair, the men . . . No. You don't want to think of that. Put that away. Stuff it in a box and close the lid.

There are plenty of other things to wonder about. Because even though each day is the same here—yesterday and tomorrow are today—you find time to wonder.

When did you first hear that there was a better place to the north? A place that held the answers to all your questions. Everything you ever needed. Everything you ever *wanted* (for those aren't the same thing, are they?).

The place is called Isa, though no one remembers where that name came from or how they know it. Only that it's been muttered again and again, like its own benediction.

When did you watch the first ship push away from the shore? You remember cheering, long ago. You remember dreaming of its triumphant return. What a homecoming it would be!

But that didn't come to pass.

More ships left as you got older.

Only the smallest children cheered by then, because they had no memory.

You watched the boats vanish into the sea. You knew that they wouldn't come back, but you hoped. Deep down, you hoped.

There was a light inside you and it filled you up. It said: Someone will make it. One of these men will be our hero.

The light faded each time a ship disappeared into the horizon.

But it shined nonetheless.

Hearts of Clouds and Rock

Toppi wailed. He curled his fists and beat the air. His cheeks were a fierce shade of red. His little feet kicked at the space around him as Veyda watched helplessly. Lalani stood beside her. Eyes round like the sun. Real life terrified her more than Lo Yuzi's tales.

Not Veyda, though. Veyda wanted to examine life from all angles. She wanted to take it apart and study it. If the plants grew, she wanted to know why. If the plants didn't grow, she wanted to know why. And if Toppi's cheeks were red and if his breaths were raspy, she wanted to know how to fix it.

That's why she'd made the salve. But the salve had run out, and there were no green leaves to make more. The sun had sucked life out of the ground.

Earlier that night, things had been mostly peaceful. Veyda and Lalani curled up on their blankets; Lalani mentioned seeing Agapito at the well, and they were talking about the Malay brothers, the upcoming Sailing Day, and which brother they thought was the most handsome (Cade, they both agreed), when they heard Toppi's cries. He screamed so loudly that the sound shot over the roofs and landed on Veyda's ears. She sat up, grabbed the last of the salve, and together the girls ran to Toppi's house.

They told Toppi's father, Maddux, and his sisters that they wanted to help calm the baby. But they knew—as did Toppi's mother, Alina—that the last of the medicine was hidden under Veyda's shirt.

There wasn't much left. Not enough to make any difference.

"What will we do?" Alina said. She clutched Veyda's shoulders as they all looked down at Toppi. Veyda was just twelve, but she was the one with the answers.

Only, she didn't have any.

Her stomach tumbled.

Her mind raced.

She picked the problem apart but had no solution.

What could she do without plants?

They all tried cradling the baby, rubbing his head, kissing his feet, but still he cried. Each wail rattled with fluid.

"I'll make more," Veyda said. "I'll come back."

Alina's face whitened. Her eyes glistened with tears. "What if it's too late?"

"It's the only choice we have," Veyda said.

"I'll help," said Lalani, her eyes still on Toppi.

Veyda laid a hand on the baby's forehead. "We'll do the best we can."

They reassured Alina again and again, then walked back into the night, with the baby's cries trailing behind them.

It was dark. The moon lit their path. Bulb flies with

their lighted tails flew around them, but other than that, they couldn't see much. Their sandals kicked dust around their sweaty ankles.

"Where will we find the plants?" asked Lalani. She whispered, as if someone was right behind them. "You said there weren't anymore."

"I don't know," said Veyda. She wiped her forehead with the back of her hand. With no rain to cool the earth, it was hot, even in the middle of the night. "They must be growing somewhere."

"What about the mountain?"

"No. It's too dangerous."

"You said you didn't believe your mother's stories."

Veyda didn't. But she *did* believe in nosy villagers who would wonder what they were doing and report them to the menyoro. She could hear them now. *That Yuzi girl, she was wandering around the foot of the mountain. What if she angers Kahna? We can't take such a risk. What would a girl be doing there, anyway? I hear she doesn't even say the benedictions.*

"I don't," Veyda said. "But that doesn't mean it isn't dangerous. Besides, would you really climb the mountain?"

"If you were with me, I would," Lalani said. She paused. "Maybe Maddux and Alina should bring Toppi back to the menyoro."

The menyoro—and only the menyoro—was in charge of healing the sick. He was considered the wisest man in the village, the cleverest of them all. If there was a question, he had the answer. If there was a dispute, he had the resolution.

He had yet to cure anyone, however.

"So he can tell them a bunch of nonsense again?" Veyda shook her head. "The menyoro's only interested in two things—being adored and being obeyed. And it seems you don't need knowledge for people to do either of those. You just need the right words."

Veyda didn't even bother to whisper.

"Shh! You shouldn't say such things," said Lalani.

They arrived back at the Yuzi house, where Hetsbi

and Lo were both still asleep, apparently unmoved by Toppi's waning cries.

"Let's change your bandage," Veyda whispered. She removed Lalani's bloodied bandage and examined her injury. "It's going to bruise even more, probably. See the blue and purple? That's the blood at the skin's surface."

"How do you know?" Lalani asked.

Veyda shrugged and wrapped a fresh cloth around Lalani's leg. "Just a guess."

"I wish my mind worked like yours," Lalani said.

"No, you don't," Veyda said, smiling. "Because then you wouldn't be Lalani."

"What's so special about that? Drum says I'm as useless as a wallecta."

"A wallecta's brain is three times the size of his," said Veyda.

Lalani laughed.

But by the time the girls were back in their blankets, with the scent of heat still on their skin, the mood had changed. Lalani stared at the ceiling. Veyda sensed she was afraid, but she wasn't sure what was bothering her. There was a lot to choose from.

"What are you thinking about, sola?" Veyda whispered.

Lalani turned on her side. She blinked. "Poor Toppi."

"Your heart is made of clouds," said Veyda.

Lalani swallowed, then turned back to the ceiling.

"If my heart is made of clouds, what is yours made of?" Lalani whispered.

Veyda chewed her lip and considered this.

"Rock," she finally said. And they giggled.

Through

Lalani walked back home after the sunrise to find her mother scrubbing her finger furiously with a wet cloth. A half-mended fishnet created a trail to her chair, as if she'd jumped up and suddenly rushed to the water basin. It only took a handful of seconds for Lalani to realize what had happened. When she did, her heart fell into her sandals.

"Mama?" she said.

The house reeked of fish.

Her mother didn't lift her head.

"Is it bad?" Lalani whispered.

She wanted her mother to shrug. *No, no, it barely*

touched the skin, see? But when Lalani joined her mother at the basin, she knew that her mother had pricked her finger deeply and dangerously. And in that moment, Lalani saw her whole life laid before her, as wide and endless as the Veiled Sea, and just as terrifying.

"It will be fine," her mother said, scrubbing, scrubbing, scrubbing. The cloth was spotted with blood. Her fingertip was pink and swollen. "It doesn't mean anything. Some women prick their fingers and never get sick. Nothing to worry about."

But it was. Oh, yes, it was. And they both knew it.

Lalani rested her hand on her mother's wrist—brown skin touching—and glared at the net on the floor. She saw the traitorous needle there, lying across it, spooled with thread.

"I'm sure it will be fine, Mama," said Lalani, even though she wasn't sure at all.

Her mother tilted her head so their foreheads touched. "You better hurry to the loomers to get the rations. I need to finish."

"But how will you do it?"

Her mother tossed the blood-soaked cloth to the side, and looked at Lalani.

"Sometimes, the only way out is through," she said.

Lalani thought of her mother's tells as she walked to the loomers. The furrow of worry on her forehead. The way she wouldn't look up. The panic in her voice.

But maybe her mother was right, and everything would be okay. It wasn't a given that she would get mender's disease.

Then again, it wasn't a given that she wouldn't.

Lalani's feet hit the dirt. The fabric under her arms dampened with sweat. She looked toward the sky. Cloudless. Bright. Quiet.

The village boys were already in school, and the fishermen were distant spots on the water. The shipbuilders worked along the opposite shore, out of view and earshot, near the Veiled Sea. Women worked the crops, hunchbacked on the horizon. Lalani turned to wave hello to the washerwomen, but they weren't out yet; their bins were dry and empty. A result of the menyoro's water rationing, perhaps.

By the time Lalani reached Bosalene's house at the foot of Mount Kahna, her throat was parched and thirsty, her leg hurt, and she couldn't stop thinking about her mother's pricked finger.

"I'm sorting the rations now," Bosalene said from her doorway. "Just a moment and I'll have yours ready."

Lalani almost followed Bosalene inside—she was desperate to talk to Mora Pasa—but then she spotted My-Shek, along with three others, in the pen, nosing at the back gate. One of the bottom latches dangled oddly from the post. It looked as if it'd been kicked. The work of the shek, no doubt. But why?

The question hardly had time to form in Lalani's mind before she knew the answer. The ground in the pen was brown and barren. Bosalene's herd wandered in the sun, circling an empty water trough and searching for fresh grass. They were so desperate that they'd tried to break the gate to reach the mountain.

"Move back now," Lalani said softly as she attempted to fix the latch. "If you wander out, you may get lost."

The shek made way for her, but they were so close that their coats tickled Lalani's arms. Once she'd refastened the gate, she rubbed My-Shek's head, then the others', one by one. Their mouths were frothy with thirst.

"I'm sorry," she said. "I know you're thirsty. I'm thirsty, too."

She sat down, sunk her fingers into the black patch on My-Shek's chest, and scratched. She looked into his round, dark eyes. My-Shek's ears folded back with pleasure.

"I'm supposed to look for plants with Veyda today," Lalani said. "But I don't know if we'll find any. I thought about going to the mountain, too. So I understand how you feel." She inhaled the scent of My-Shek—thick and familiar—and whispered, "My mother pricked her finger, My-Shek. I don't know what to do."

The heat was unbearable, but she spent several

minutes there, resisting the urge to cry into the downiness of My-Shek's coat, waiting for Bosalene to appear with the basket of thread. Eventually, though, the heat was too much, and she stood to walk back to the house. She was halfway there, brushing dirt from her shirt, when she discovered that her attempt to fix the gate had been a failure. It was wide open.

My-Shek and two others had already wandered out and were walking up the slope.

There was no time to get Bosalene. By the time Lalani made it to the house and back again, who knew how far the shek would go? They were moving fast already, certainly faster than Lalani thought shek could move.

Lalani hesitated, glanced over her shoulder, then hurried to the broken gate. She closed it, hands fumbling, so the others wouldn't escape. She needed to get the loose shek before they went too far. She stepped quickly toward the mountain, only to find that she could no longer see the animals.

But there—in the distance. Was that My-Shek?

Something moved, that was certain, but she couldn't tell if it was one of the shek or not.

Poor My-Shek! If he wandered too far, he would never find his way back. None of them would. What if they were snatched by the mountain beast? Or some other creature? And without the shek, the loomers wouldn't be able to make enough thread. And without enough thread, her mother wouldn't be able to mend. All things considered, that didn't sound like such a terrible fate, but when you didn't meet expectations, your rations were lowered by the menyoro, which meant less food. She could see Drum now, glaring at their meager serving of fish and vegetables, his eyes hooded under dark brows.

She took a step forward.

Yes, that was My-Shek.

She glanced back toward the house.

Her heart thundered.

She recalled the voice of Lo Yuzi. The story of the mountain beast.

Mount Kahna doesn't wish to be disturbed! It will eat you alive!

But she had no choice—did she? She had to get the shek before they went too far.

They were probably hiding behind that cluster of trees or grazing lazily in a shadow.

She had to at least *try* to find them.

I won't go too far. Just far enough.

Whispering the Sanlagitan benediction under her breath—*Spare us. Remain peaceful and quiet in our gratitude*—she stepped toward the mountain.

Shifty

Nature is shifty. It takes advantage of how comfortable you are in your surroundings. Humans make the mistake of believing they know best, but nature is there to remind you, at precisely the wrong time, that nature was here first.

Lalani wasn't in the habit of believing she knew best about anything. She had never been deep in a forest's belly. She certainly had never been on the slope of a mountain.

She followed My-Shek cautiously at first, but then became so focused on bringing all of the shek home that she forgot to be afraid. She called to them—"Here, shek, here, shek"—but they didn't come. They bowed their heads to the grassy slope and nosed around for food. When Lalani got close enough to grab one by the loose skin around his neck, he shook her off and they all hurried away.

She followed them. She didn't think about how long she'd been walking until she noticed that her feet ached and she saw a tree with golden leaves. Had she seen such a tree before? How far had she come, anyway?

Bosalene and the loomers were behind her somewhere. But then, why couldn't she see the pitched roofs of their houses, or any houses for that matter?

She looked up, up, up. The trees stretched on forever. And the sky was growing dark. Not as dark as midnight, no. But the world around her was gray. She hadn't noticed that until now. The tree canopy blocked the sun. It was still hot, but not as overwhelming as before. In any other circumstance, she would have taken comfort in that.

She hugged herself and turned around. The shek were still visible, oblivious to the danger they were in. (They *were* in danger, weren't they?) She spun in slow circles.

Even if she corralled the shek, how would she lead them back? Why hadn't she thought this through?

It was so quiet. There was no wind to rustle the leaves. No birds flitting from branch to branch. Just the sound of her breathing and the muffled sound of the shek eating.

"It's okay," she told them, though they didn't seem to need comforting. "You didn't go far."

She had no idea if that was true or not.

She stopped spinning.

She had no idea what to do. She had no idea what her next step should be. She stood still, waiting for an answer, even though she didn't know where it would come from. Maybe the mountain beast would give her one, just before he gobbled them all up. An image popped into her mind. An ugly image. The mountain beast, coming after her with sharp, hungry teeth. Mouth frothing like the shek's—from hunger, not thirst. And his claws. Oh, his claws! Then, a growl. *Your eyes. Your eyessssss.* Because that's what the mountain beast wanted. That's what he always wanted.

Eyes for his supper.

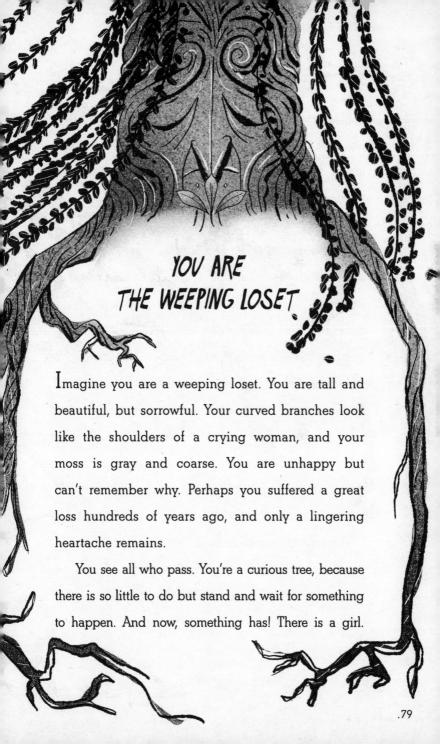

YOU ARE
THE WEEPING LOSET

Imagine you are a weeping loset. You are tall and beautiful, but sorrowful. Your curved branches look like the shoulders of a crying woman, and your moss is gray and coarse. You are unhappy but can't remember why. Perhaps you suffered a great loss hundreds of years ago, and only a lingering heartache remains.

You see all who pass. You're a curious tree, because there is so little to do but stand and wait for something to happen. And now, something has! There is a girl.

You've never seen her before. She smells hot and dry, like dust. She steps lightly, but purposefully, and she is afraid. You know this because your roots plunge into the earth, and everything that touches the ground settles onto them.

Her eyes are wide. She studies you. She doesn't understand why you're here, and you don't understand, either. Her eyes are frightened. You've been afraid before, too. You remember that now. You ache to comfort her. You think: *If my arms were stronger, I would lower them for her to climb. She could make a bed from my leaves and rest here until morning.* But your arms aren't strong enough to carry a girl, especially one who is burdened by exhaustion and fear. Those things are the heaviest of all. And you are just an old loset covered with moss.

Few people pass through here. Just the eyeless man. But this girl has eyes, certainly. They are inquisitive, like they carry a thousand questions. You have no answers.

You decide to rustle your leaves so she knows you see her.

There. You blew her hair, but too lightly. You don't have much strength anymore.

You think: *Maybe she is afraid of the eyeless man. Maybe that is where her fear comes from.* And she's right to be afraid. *Poor thing,* you think, *she's just a girl.* You've lived three hundred years, and she's only lived a handful.

How tragic.

She will never know the comfort of your branches.

You think: *I could be a hero to you, girl, if only I were different. But this is what I am. So you are doomed.*

Then They Strike

"I'm not afraid," said Lalani. She shivered among the trees, even though it was very warm. "I'm not afraid."

She was, of course. But if you can trick yourself, sometimes you wind up believing something that isn't true. Lo Yuzi had taught Lalani that one night, when she and Veyda hadn't been able to sleep because they were thinking about their fathers. They had been ten years old and wondering about their papas' journey together. How far did they get before their ship sank? What were they thinking? Did they suffer? It was a terrible conversation and it made their hearts clench, but they couldn't help themselves. Eventually they'd burst into tears, and Lo Yuzi had come in to see what was wrong.

Sometimes you must feel pain, she'd said, stroking their hair. *But when you tire from it, tell yourself: I will be okay. I will survive. Even if you don't believe it. Eventually, you will. Because it was never a lie to begin with. You will. We all will.*

Lalani tried that now.

"I'm not afraid," she said.

She wished she were more like Veyda or Ziva.

She waited for her feet to move more bravely, but they didn't. She took small, uncertain steps, her knee throbbing faintly with each of them. Everything around her was both frighteningly identical and completely unfamiliar.

"I will be okay," she said.

She thought of Veyda, who never seemed afraid of anything. Perhaps it was something she inherited from Lo Yuzi. But no—that couldn't be right, because Hetsbi was also born from Lo Yuzi, and there wasn't a more frightened boy in the village.

She thought of Ziva, so bold that she hid away on a ship.

But Ziva hadn't made it, Lalani reminded herself. And even Veyda was afraid of the mountain. Too scared to look for plants on its slopes.

Oh, yes, the plants. Lalani scanned the ground around her. There was green here, certainly, and not just the grass being eaten by the sheks. There were also plants that spiked in all directions, others with flat round leaves, still others with furry oval ones. Plants that sprouted around the roots of trees and those that grew alone. The trouble was, Lalani had no clue which ones Veyda needed. She debated whether she should gather some or focus on the task at hand—the shek. Perhaps she could do both. She leaned over. Plucked a handful. The leaves were dry, but not wilted. She felt better. Yes, she was still lost. Yes, she was still afraid. But at least she had a purpose.

We all need a purpose, her mother liked to say. *That's why we must be thankful for the menyoro.*

Then, another ugly thought: her mother's finger. The bloody cloth. The needle.

Don't think about that now.

"I'll keep gathering plants," Lalani said to no one. "And let the shek eat their fill."

Her gathering soon led her to the roots of a magnificent tree, one Lalani had certainly never seen before—not on this day or any other. It was tall, stately, and dripping with moss. Its branches were spindly but curved. The tree looked like it was crying. A faint breeze blew from its leaves, the first one Lalani had felt in days. It was as if the tree was trying to comfort her. And even if that didn't make sense, Lalani didn't care. She would take comfort wherever she could.

Soon after Kul became Lalani's brother, he told her that spirits of dead menders rose from their graves at night and slipped between the flenka boards in the walls. He'd kneel beside her to whisper his tale. His voice was the only sound in the world.

"They stink, and their brains hang out of their ears. They wear seaweed and grass capes and carry needles that are four feet long," he would say. "They come in through the cracks, but you can't see them because they're invisible. They can always tell who has the weakest spirit in the room so they know who to attack. That's why I don't have to worry. But if I were you, I'd be scared. You have a weak spirit, even for a girl. They'll choke you to death. They wait for the silence of night. Then they strike." He wrapped his hands around his own neck to demonstrate.

Lalani knew Kul wanted to scare her and that it probably wasn't true, but she was scared nonetheless. She couldn't sleep when it was quiet, so she'd focus on the deep breaths of her mother. But then she would start to worry that her mother would get mender's disease and come back as a ghost, and eventually she grew to fear her own sleeping mother.

How was it, she wondered, that Lo Yuzi's stories thrilled her, but Kul's made her afraid of her own mama?

After weeks of fitful sleep, Lalani finally told her mother about Kul's story.

"Why would mothers come back to haunt the

children?" her mother had said, shaking her head. "No, mothers wouldn't do such a thing, even in death. If dead menders were to haunt anyone, it would be Kul."

Her mother rarely said such things, so this both surprised and comforted Lalani. After that, the story drifted from her memory, almost as if she'd never heard it.

But now, as she stood in the complete silence of Mt. Kahna, old fears blossomed.

The world wasn't saying a word.

They wait for the silence. . . . Then they strike.

One foot in front of the other. That's what she had to do. She turned around and retraced her steps—or she thought she did.

"I'm not afraid," said Lalani.

The shek had wandered off. A sickening feeling swirled in Lalani's belly. The shek were nowhere in sight. *My-Shek* was nowhere in sight. She'd wanted to take care of them, and she'd failed. As useless as a wallecta, just like Drum said.

No. She would make herself useful. She would keep

hold of the plants and try to find her way. She would *not* think about her tired feet, her hurt knee, or all the things that could snatch her. Mountain beasts. Mender ghosts. The mountain itself.

She wasn't going to think about the boy with the canteen, the boy who ignored everyone's warnings and traipsed up Kahna alone, never to be seen again.

She wished it wasn't so quiet.

Her feet crunched the dry leaves. *Crunch, crunch*.

She pictured her mother's face, then Lo Yuzi, and Veyda. Something to comfort her.

Mountains are mountains.

She stopped and looked around. Where was that weeping tree? She'd felt some degree of comfort near it. Maybe she should sit under its canopy and figure out what to do next.

Crunch, crunch.

She squeezed her eyes shut and opened them, willing all the bad thoughts away.

"I am not afraid," she said. Louder this time. "I am

not afraid." She raised her fists in the air—one of them stuffed with plants—and said, "I am a mighty warrior! I will conquer this mountain! Beware all who wish to stop me!"

Her heart sprinted through her chest.

She pulled a dangling twig from a nearby tree and swung it in front of her. The twig was shaped like an ax-saw, sort of. It had a curved tip, like a hook.

Whoosh-whoosh. Her whipping branch cut through the quiet.

But then she heard something else, too.

What was that?

She dropped the twig. There. Very faint. *Bz-bzz-bz.* Something winked at her, a pinprick of light. Only one at first, then another and another.

A bulb fly. Three of them. Little fluttering insects with lighted wings. Despite her precarious situation, Lalani couldn't help but feel a rush of excitement. She loved bulb flies!

Lalani followed them without thinking about it. They shined bright and hopeful, even though it wasn't yet dark. Soon she reached a creek, where she fell to her knees and drank greedily. She hadn't realized how thirsty she was. She drank and drank and drank, even though some of the handfuls she scooped from the creek were spotted with dirt and it caught in her throat and made her cough. The creek was thin and unimpressive, slivering along the earth like a worm. Still, it was water. She hoped My-Shek had—or would—find it.

The bulb flies were gone now, so she followed the creek. Lo Yuzi had told her once that water was life. And she was right. Without the rain, life was precarious. Perhaps this creek led to a roaring river. It didn't appear so, but things weren't always what they seemed.

The air cooled enough to remind her that she was far from home. Far from her mother. Far from Veyda. Lost.

The trees were thicker. Denser.

"Mountains are of no threat to me!" she said. "The mountain is not as tall as my spirit!"

She wished she'd kept the twig. She reached out, hoping to find another branch, but the meha trees were too massive and hearty to leave loose pieces behind.

"I am as strong as the meha!"

But she knew she wasn't.

She turned to the west. At least she thought it was west. At some point the creek had abandoned her. But she was not alone. A hushed noise, like a sigh. It was the rustling of leaves. She kept moving, and that's when she saw it: the tree of weeping moss. It was here again! Progress.

With the next step, another sound. Not a sigh. No, nothing like that. A snarl. Growl. Hiss. A wide mouth opening. Hot breath on her neck. Drops of frothy saliva landing on her shoulders.

Her heart stopped. Her feet, too.

She thought: run.

But she couldn't move. And when she finally could, two clawed hands rose up and snatched her.

Eyes

"Do you know how lucky you are?"

The words came from far away. It was a man's voice. Deep and throaty. Lalani's eyes were closed, and she was afraid to open them. She wiggled her fingers and toes. She was in one piece. But what had happened?

The air around her was stale and unmoving. She was indoors. She knew, too, that she was on a floor made of wood. Flenka, perhaps.

Had she made it back to the village somehow?

She heard a noise. *Clop-clop-clop.* Then closer. *Clop-shh. Clop-shh.* Slowly, slowly. Near her ear now. Her heart leaped awake and banged in her chest.

"You were nearly killed," the man said.

She sat up quickly and scurried back as fast as she could, until there was nowhere else for her to go. Standing in front of her, like a tower, like a soaring spike of rock, was a man with two enormous horns, curved horns that sat atop his head, horns that ended in two sharp points, horns that looked so heavy that Lalani wondered how he carried them. But that wasn't what frightened her most—although it certainly was frightening, yes, to see a man with horns—no, what frightened her most was his face.

He had no eyes.

"I sense your fear," he said. "But there's no need to be afraid. I won't hurt you. I saved your life. You were about to be killed by the beast who lives in these mountains."

The house was small. Just one room. The man leaned on a broken and whittled branch—an unusual-looking cane that seemed to sparkle. A small pouch dangled around his neck. Lalani glanced to her left: a table topped with slivers of tree bark. A single chair, with a blanket draped across it.

Lalani swallowed. She pushed herself against the wall.

The man stood there, quietly balancing on his cane, his chin dipping toward her as if he could see. His white hair was dirty and matted around his horns. She saw now that he had a beard. That was matted, too.

"The beast?" said Lalani.

He nodded once. "There are beasts everywhere." He paused. "What is your name?"

She hesitated. She pressed her palms against the floor.

"I'd rather not say," she replied.

"I'll just call you Girl, then," he said. He straightened up as much as he could. "My name is Ellseth."

Lalani's mind scrambled. Had Lo Yuzi ever told a story about a man with horns named Ellseth? No, she didn't think so. She'd told them about a beast without eyes, though. And this man certainly had no eyes. But he looked too old and tired to be a beast.

It was impossible to sort out. If there was indeed a man in the mountain who had no eyes, then it must also be true that there was a man in the mountain who had no eyes and wanted to eat hers for supper. Right? Was it possible for there to be two truths? Or half-truths? How was she to know?

She wished Veyda was with her.

"Ellseth," Lalani repeated.

She felt better knowing he had a name, at least. It was harder to fear someone who had a name.

"You must be from the village below the mountain," he said. He turned and lumbered to the single chair, finding his way with the cane. He groaned as he sat. "I've never been there. I can't travel far, as you can imagine." He waved toward his face. "Not anymore, anyway."

Lalani took a deep, deep breath. Her heart slowed. Her mind still whispered *danger, danger*, but she managed to quiet it. It would be easy to escape this room, after all.

Then again, if she escaped—how would she find her way home?

And what if the beast attacked her again?

She cleared her throat. "Do you know the way back to the village?"

He rested both wrinkled hands atop his cane. "I'm afraid not. I know little of where I am or how long I've been here."

"You were not born of Kahna?"

"What is 'Kahna'?"

"This mountain, which watches over us."

"Kahna," he said, as if he wanted to try the word on his tongue.

"If you are not from the mountain, or the village, then where did you come from?"

Lalani had never seen anyone who wasn't from Sanlagita. The Sanlagitans, after all, had no idea what, if anything, existed beyond their island. Their legends told them there was an island to the north, across the Veiled Sea, but that was all they knew. The idea that this man (was it a man or a creature?) was from somewhere other than Sanlagita or Mount Kahna seemed as mysterious and bewildering as the notion of singing birds. Lalani's curiosity swelled until it overshadowed her fear and the voice whispering *danger, danger.*

"I come from Isa," said Ellseth.

A gasp lodged in Lalani's throat. So many men had died—including her father, and Veyda's—searching for Isa, wondering if it existed, and here was this horned man telling her he'd been there.

Was he lying? Lalani searched for tells, but they were difficult to spot.

"Isa?" she said.

"Yes, of course."

"How?"

"How what?"

How what? How everything. There were so many questions fighting for her attention that she didn't know which one to ask.

Veyda always said that when you have a problem, you should ask the most obvious question first.

"Why are you here?" Lalani asked.

Ellseth breathed deep. It rattled in his chest. His shoulders fell, no longer proud. He lowered his chin. Lalani could see that there were patches where his horns had peeled, as if they had also wrinkled and aged.

"I was banished," he said. "As punishment for my misdeeds."

Just like in Lo Yuzi's story.

You spend your days all alone, dreaming of your other life, when you had friends and family. But you know that this life is what you're due, because of all your sins.

Lalani's eyes widened.

"There are two kinds of children," Ellseth said. "Those who delight in stories and those who are too afraid to listen." He lifted his chin and leaned toward Lalani. The chair creaked beneath him. "Do you delight in stories?"

Lalani swallowed. "I do."

Ellseth tapped his cane against the floor. *Clop.*

"Then I will tell you mine," he said.

Ellseth's Story

I was once a boy. A child, like you. My kind are called the mindoren. Have you heard of the mindoren before? No, I suppose not. But we roam everywhere on Isa. We are on the hills. The mountain slopes. The meadows and flatlands. I've not seen your island—of course, I haven't—but mine? Isa? It is lush and alive. The mindoren are peaceful, but solitary. And although I was a good boy, with no wicked thoughts in my head, the solitude and idleness worked tricks on me. I began to wonder what else this life could give me, and I wanted more. More happiness. More joy. All the time, more. I fell asleep under the dark blanket of night with that word dancing through my dreams. More, more, more. There is only one way to have more. You must take from someone else. Because to have more, there needs to be less. How else would we measure "more"?

Do you understand?

I sense that you are a child who doesn't ask for more.

I was not such a child.

I became a thief.

Small treasures, at first. A berry from someone else's basket or a dish from someone else's bedside. But when that was no longer enough, I took handfuls. Then baskets. I had everything I needed, but I wanted more. There is a difference between "want" and "need."

You understand. Perhaps the curse of the mindoren is that they have all they need. What is left to do but want?

But that's the funny thing, Girl—the others? They didn't want like I did. Mindoren are peaceful and kind. It's in their nature. But somehow, it wasn't in *my* nature. I became combative. I pulled at my horns when I didn't get what I wanted. Why should my neighbor have more wonderful things than I did, when my neighbor was no better than me? Why should I have to spend afternoons picking another basket of berries when there are baskets already full? Yes, I know those berries belonged to someone else, but if they truly wanted them, they should have taken better care of them.

But berries aren't enough for a thief.

I took more chances.

I took many things. Valuable things. Things I will never speak of.

I took them from powerful creatures, far more powerful than the mindoren. It made me feel powerful, too. I walked with my head held high. At first I hid my treasures away but found that it's no use being powerful if no one can admire your power. I wanted people to know what I had done, to respect me, my cunning, my prowess, my trickery.

Gradually I revealed my treasures. Look at this, I would say. I stole this from the great creature of the sea. And this, taken from the nest of the bai. Look how powerful I am. Look how you should fear me.

What a fool I was, Girl.

The mindoren are not fearful, after all.

They are peaceful.

I've said that, haven't I?

Instead of respecting me and admiring my stolen treasures, the mindoren took me while I was sleeping and tied my body to a tree. They tied my horns, too, so I couldn't move my head.

"I'm not afraid of you!" I cried.

But I'll tell you a secret, Girl. I *was* afraid. Because one of the elders approached me then. He held a wooden spike in his hand. Our noses were nearly touching. I could smell his breath. He tapped the spike against my temple.

"Your greed touches everything your eyes fall upon," he said. "And now your eyes shall fall to the ground."

His face was the last thing I saw, Girl. I remember every inch of it, from his horns to his chin. I'm sure he is dead now, for he was old then. How effortlessly he took my sight! As if he'd stolen a thousand eyes before mine.

Maybe he had.

The pain was so great that I no longer remember it. I must have slept, right there lashed to the tree. When I woke, I didn't know where I was. I couldn't see. Oh, how I screamed. *Where am I? Where am I?* I knew right away I was in exile. We often spoke of an island to the south, infested with vicious creatures, and certainly that was where they'd sent me.

I am a mindoren, and I know my kind; therefore, three things are certain.

One: They wanted to make it impossible for me to move freely about the world.

Two: They did not want to take care of me after they gouged out my eyes, for mindoren live many, many years.

Three: They did not have the heart to kill me.

Mindorens are peaceful, after all.

It took me a long time to realize how wrong I was to act as I did, to covet power and possessions. And I've considered how I could repay my debts, even to my own conscience. But how can a man who lives alone, who survives on berries and bark and can barely go outside his home, do this? I am kind to the trees, but trees don't ask for much. To whom can I offer kindnesses to ease my conscience?

And then, I found you. Though I cannot see you, I sense your goodness and light. I sense that you are deserving.

I saved you from the beast, yes, and that was good. You can leave here with your life, and what greater gift is that? But I've committed many wrongs, Girl. One deed, however tremendous and noble, is not enough.

I'd like to do something else for you.

I'd like to grant you a wish.

Provided I can.

There are limits, certainly. But I still wield much power.

Tell me—what do you wish for?

I sense your hesitation. But remember, Girl: you can trust me.

You can trust me with your life.

Just Such a Girl

Lalani never looked away from Ellseth. This was a story of a different sort, because this one was true. This man had lived on Isa. He'd been tied to a tree. His eyes were gone. He sat before her with horns on his head.

What would Veyda do?

Start with the most obvious question first.

"How would you grant my wish?" she asked. She sat forward, legs crossed, with her elbows on her knees. "Do you have magical powers?"

"The mindoren have no magical powers," he said. "But I still have the udyo."

"What is the udyo?"

He tapped his finger against his cane and coughed. "A token of magic. One of the items I took during my days as a thief. I had it hidden when they banished me, and they never discovered it."

Oh, how she wished Veyda and Hetsbi were here! They'd never believe her when she told them. And what would Lo Yuzi say? Not only had Lalani gone into the mountain, she'd been attacked by the beast and then saved by a horned creature with a magical cane! Lalani had never done anything brave, and she wasn't sure if she was being brave now. Still, this was a story to tell.

"But—" Lalani hesitated. "How do I *know* you can actually do magic with the . . . udyo?"

Ellseth shrugged. "Give me a small test."

Lalani bit her bottom lip and looked around the room. Should she ask him to make something fly? Make one of those slivers of bark rise in the air, perhaps? No. This was his house—what if he'd planted tricks? It had to be something that she *knew* was magic.

"Can you heal the wound on my knee?" she asked. If he could do that, she would know he was telling the truth.

"Of course," Ellseth said.

He rubbed his hand over his cane and lifted his chin.

"But wait," said Lalani. "If you can heal my knee, how come you don't heal your eyes?"

Aha. She'd tricked him! Veyda would be proud.

"The udyo isn't able to create something from nothing, Girl," he said. He leaned forward, leveling his eyeless face at her. His voice lowered to a throaty whisper. "And as you can see—I have nothing."

Lalani's heart stopped.

She swallowed.

"Any other questions?" he asked.

She shook her head, even though she knew he couldn't see her.

"Let's get on with it, then," he said, his knuckles white from gripping his cane.

Lalani wasn't sure what she expected. She hadn't had

time to expect anything, really. What did it feel like to have magic performed on you? It felt like a faint buzz, a trembling of bones, a wash of light. A jolt of fear. The stitching of skin. Stitch-stitch-stitch. Like the skillful hands of a village mender. Like her mother.

And then: Strange images that made no sense. A single tree. The piercing scream of a girl. Words. *My udyo! My udyo!* And here was a man with wide, light eyes. Sparkling circles that glinted mischief. A devilish twist in his mouth. Hands outstretched, reaching—but not *his* hands, no. The girl's. *My udyo! My udyo!*

Stitch-stitch-stitch.

Those eyes. That mouth. Was it Ellseth? No. This man was young and crafty.

Just as he had been, once upon a time.

Right?

Stitch-stitch-stitch.

There was not a moment to consider it, because the throbbing pain in her knee lifted and the images drifted away, like smoke.

She knew the wound was gone even before she removed the scrap of fabric.

Her skin was unbroken. Unbruised.

As if she had never fallen.

Lalani was so amazed that the image of the man and the girl disappeared as quickly as it'd come.

"Can you heal my mother?" she asked.

"Perhaps, but you must bring her here," answered Ellseth. "The udyo can only manipulate things within sight."

A strange choice of words, Lalani thought.

"I can't bring my mother here," she said. Her mother would never agree to it, no matter how much Lalani begged. And her mother could fall sick any day now. How would she make the journey?

What, then?

She thought of Toppi. A baby would be easy to carry. She could wish for him to get better. But what good would that do? If it wasn't Toppi, it would be someone else. Other menders would still prick their fingers. Other babies would still develop fevers. Her mother would still die. She wanted to save Toppi, but she wanted to save her mother, too. She wanted to save everyone. But how?

"There is another catch to our deal, Girl," Ellseth said. "You can't tell anyone I'm here. You must swear."

Lalani wasn't accustomed to keeping secrets. And this would be the greatest secret of all. How could she hide it from Veyda?

"If the villagers know I'm here, they will hunt me down and kill me," Ellseth said.

"They won't," Lalani replied.

Ellseth pulled the udyo close and leaned forward, forward, closing the space between them.

"You must swear," he said again. And if he'd had eyes, Lalani was sure they would have glowed with fury.

Still, he had saved her from a monster.

If he wanted to hurt her, why would he have saved her?

Yes, he had once been a thief. But now he wanted to make things right. He wanted to grant one wish to someone deserving.

And she was just such a girl.

"I swear," she said.

Ellseth smiled and leaned back again. "Do you know what you wish for, Girl?"

"Yes," said Lalani. "I wish for rain."

Three Drops

Lalani swore her secrecy to Ellseth, and he agreed to make rain. When he walked to the nearby table, she followed. He removed the pouch from his neck, pulled it open with a swift push of his spindly finger, and removed a sharp, shiny object.

"What is that?" she asked.

"You've never seen an arrowhead before?" asked Ellseth, his brows furrowed. He turned it around in his palm. "How do your people hunt? How do your people eat?"

"We eat fish from the southern sea. And we eat the

shek when their coats are no longer useful to us." Lalani thought of My-Shek and the others. Where were they now? Had they made it home?

"You cannot survive on Isa without an arrowhead," Ellseth said.

"Is it dangerous there? The stories always made it sound—"

"It's dangerous everywhere," Ellseth interrupted. "Danger lurks in dark places. Danger lurks in beautiful places. You can never escape it."

Lalani swallowed. "Is it true that there is a mountain on Isa full of life's good fortunes?"

"Yes, it is true."

"Is it true that a yellow flower grows there? A yellow flower with specks of white?"

"Fei Diwata has a garden of flowers, but I never cared what they looked like."

"Where is Fei Diwata and what does the mountain look like?"

Ellseth placed a sliver of tree bark between them. His

fingers moved expertly, as if he'd memorized every inch of his house.

"You ask too many questions, Girl. Now give me your hand."

Lalani was so caught up in her questions that she laid her hand on his without hesitation. Her mouth was barely able to keep up with her mind. "What are the fortunes? What happens when you get there?"

"Fei Diwata isn't a *place*, Girl. Fei Diwata is a creature. She lives on the mountain, where everything good exists," he said. "But Fei Diwata hoards it for herself. That is why there is so much misery. She refuses to share. I always considered it foolish that she should be the one to guard the mountain. Why her? I was just as equal to the task."

Lalani thought of her mother's pierced finger. Her father's disappearance in his search for Isa. Toppi's pink cheeks. The menyoro's men guarding the pump because there wasn't enough water.

And she thought of this vicious creature, keeping everything good for herself.

"Has anyone talked to Fei Diwata? Has anyone told her of all the misery?"

Ellseth huffed. "Fei Diwata is useless." He fumbled with the arrowhead. "A drop of blood in exchange for your wish, and your oath."

And before Lalani could protest, he sliced her thumb and squeezed three fat drops of blood onto the bark.

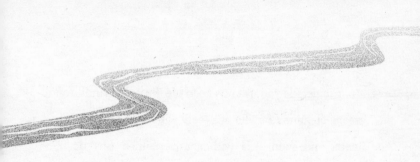

YOU ARE THE NALUPAI

Imagine you have two islands in a vast ocean. You watch over them. They are yours, yes, but you have enough already. You are kind and generous, and don't believe in keeping more than you need. So, you decide: you will give them away.

In the land above, where you exist, there are many others like you. Collectively, you are called the Nalupai. The Nalupai are peaceful and loving. Look at the beautiful trees below, the Nalupai whisper proudly to one another. Look how the wind blows. Look how the grass bends. Look at the magnificent colors.

You decide your islands need life. But what kind? You create creatures for the sea—eels with beautiful human heads and mermaids with sharp pointed fins down their backs. You create magnificent birds for the trees and herds of horned beasts to roam the countryside. You make mountains. Fish. Quiet animals with shelled backs. And you think: yes, this is beautiful. But how do you maintain balance? Your wish is for all creatures to delight in happiness, so you create a Diwata to watch over them. You name her Fei. You tell her, *These islands belong to those who possess life's greatest virtue.* You whisper that virtue in her ear—one word. And she smiles and nods and stares at you with her new, sparkling eyes. You give her all of life's good fortunes and say—*Guard this. Be protective of it. Don't allow anyone to steal it.*

You give her the udyo to help her with this task.

Do you see that tree there? you ask her. It's a tree you created. It looks ordinary, but you know that ordinary things aren't always what they seem.

Yes, Mother Nalupai, she says.

I will place it on a great mountain, you tell her. *And you will climb into it. You will keep the udyo with you always. Do you understand?*

Yes, Mother Nalupai, Fei Diwata says.

You know there will be problems, of course. You cannot place living things together without expecting some problems. But you embrace this reality with both magical arms, because without pain, there is no joy. How do you know you are happy if you don't know what it means to be sad?

Fei Diwata does not protect the islands alone. There are others, such as the eel-woman. She is protective of her water. She creates a veil to prevent passage. Great swarms of witches weave hives from the branches of your trees. But still, you are not worried. This is what life is. There is joy, there is pain. There is good, there is evil. Such is the way of things. So, happy with your creations, you leave them be.

You have last words for Fei Diwata: *Take care of what I've created here.* And then you are gone, like a whisper.

Hetsbi the Believer

Hetsbi should have never believed the Pasa boys when they said they wanted him to join their secret workers guild, but they'd looked so sincere. And being friends with Bio and Dah Pasa seemed like a much better deal than being their target. He knew what that was like.

"Come on," said Bio as they gathered their few belongings to walk back to the village after school. The boys had pulled him aside, away from the others—although, truth be told, Hetsbi was often away from the others—to tell him about their plan.

The heat beat down on them. Sweat lined their faces,

but they were used to it, so they didn't brush it away. Cade was several paces ahead of them, alone and lost in his thoughts. It was unlike Cade to be alone, but ever since the menyoro had announced that his brother would sail . . . well, it was enough to weigh on anyone.

"We'll just help each other with our assignments," said Bio. "That way we can all get high marks and won't get stuck fishing."

"Bio and I want to become shipbuilders," Dah said. "Don't you, Hetsbi?"

Of course. Every boy wanted the menyoro to make him a shipbuilder. It wasn't as admirable as being a sailor, but at least you didn't die.

"Yes," Hetsbi answered, quietly. "But . . ."

"But what?" asked Dah.

"Yes," said Bio. "But what?"

Everyone knows I couldn't even build a simple scouting boat. I can barely even fish.

He opened his mouth to say just that, then closed it again. He wasn't sure why the Pasa boys were suddenly being nice to him, but he didn't want to ruin it by reminding them who he was.

"There's just one thing you have to do," Dah said. He traded a quick, mischievous glance with his brother.

"Yes," Bio agreed. "It's a small test, but we're making everyone do it. You're the first. Next is Cade. He already agreed."

Hetsbi looked at Cade, who was too far away to hear them, his ax-saw bumping against his leg, sweat staining his shirt.

"Really?" Hetsbi said. "Cade agreed?"

"Oh, sure," said Bio. "And when you're done, we'll be able to tell him that you went first and weren't afraid. Unless . . . "

Hetsbi swallowed. "Unless what?"

"Unless you *are* afraid."

"I'm not afraid," said Hetsbi, much too quickly.

But he was.

Of course he was.

Under the Cloudless Sky

Veyda found Toppi's mother sitting on the rocks, staring blankly at the fishing boats that dotted the sea in the distance. Toppi was nestled in her arms. The pink in his cheeks had developed into a spotted rash.

Veyda sat beside them.

"He's quiet now," Toppi's mother said, without turning away from the water. Her voice was weary and hoarse, like she hadn't slept in weeks. "It frightens me."

"I know," Veyda said. "I'm sorry."

It wasn't her fault—she couldn't *force* the plants to grow—but she felt as if she had failed, nonetheless.

She was the one who made the salve, and now she had nothing to clear Toppi's lungs and make him feel better. She'd searched for plants, but there were none to find. They were all dying under the cloudless sky. Lalani had never showed up to help her look—odd, but not alarming, considering all the tasks girls were asked to do for their mothers at the last minute—but it wouldn't have mattered anyway.

"It's still possible he will recover," said Veyda. "Perhaps that's why he's quiet now. Because he's feeling better."

But he didn't look better.

He looked much worse.

"Perhaps," Toppi's mother said. She glanced down at her son. A tear plopped on his forehead. "When I was a little girl, my papa told me that wallecta know when they're going to die. They burrow into their souls and go quietly." She looked up, eyes glistening. "Do you think that's what is happening with my Toppi? Is he going quietly?"

The weight on Veyda's chest was so heavy that she found it difficult to speak.

She wanted to say no. She wanted to say that Toppi would recover and live a long, happy life. She wanted to say she had a bowl of salve waiting for him.

But Veyda lived in a world of truth, and she believed in it fiercely.

"I hope not," she said. And she kissed the baby's speckled cheek.

Stand Right Here

The Pasa brothers brought Hetsbi to a spot near the base of Mount Kahna.

"What about the menyoro?" asked Hetsbi.

The menyoro's house was within eyesight, a notable distance from the village to signify the menyoro's importance. The Pasa home was near here as well, because they tended to the shek, though Bosalene—the boys' mother—often implied that it was their superiority, not the sheks' diet, that brought them closer to the menyoro and the mountain.

The boys ignored Hetsbi's question. They stepped

into the weeds and waved for Hetsbi to follow.

He didn't want to.

Not one bit.

He feared the mountain. That's why he said his benediction every night. Not as a chore, but with every meaningful breath in his body. And now here they were, standing in Kahna's shadow.

"Don't worry," Dah said, waving his brown hand impatiently toward Hetsbi. "We're not going up the mountain. You just need to come stand right here."

"Yes," Bio said. He looked into the weeds, at something near his feet. "The initiation ceremony is right here."

Hetsbi wasn't a fool.

He knew how the Pasa boys were.

They were mean. Vengeful. They made other people the target of their jokes, and their jokes were never funny to anyone but them.

Even though he knew all these things about Dah and Bio, even though every beat of his heart told him this whole scenario was a bad idea, he did not run away.

He didn't say *never mind, I don't want to join your guild after all.* He didn't say *I know you two are up to something and I want no part of it.* Because there was a pinprick of possibility—smaller than a bulb fly, smaller than the tip of a mending needle—that this was real and true. That maybe this, whatever this was, would be a chance for him to show them a remarkable display of bravery that they would never forget.

He lifted one foot, then the other. It was difficult to walk, but he did. Just a few steps.

He didn't see what was in the weeds until he was standing between the Pasa brothers.

A baby pahaalusk looked up at them from the scorched grass. Peels of dry skin stretched over its shell. A line of froth dripped from its mouth. Thirst.

Hetsbi felt every hair on his body.

"Dah found it yesterday on our way to school," Bio said proudly. "It was walking behind its mother."

The boys laughed, though Hetsbi didn't see the joke in it.

Pahaalusk were common on the island. They lived mostly along the shore or among the plants or trees. Their meat was too tough to eat and their shells were nearly impossible to crack. Pahaalusk survived on grass— although who knew for how much longer, without the rain?—alongside the Sanlagitans, who had little use for them. Hetsbi had never found them particularly endearing.

"He took it," Bio added, still with a note of pride.

"Took it?" Hetsbi said.

Dah crossed his arms. "I just picked it up. Stupid thing didn't even struggle. Then I brought it here."

"Talk about stupid," Bio agreed. He toed the pahaalusk with his sandal. "He hasn't even moved."

"But . . ." Hetsbi began. He wasn't sure he would manage the next word, but he did: "Why?"

The Pasa brothers turned to him, eyebrows furrowed.

"Why?" Dah repeated, as if it were the most ridiculous question he'd ever heard.

"For the initiation," Bio said. "Of course."

Hetsbi felt every bead of sweat. Every beat of his heart.

"What do you want me to do?" he asked.

Hetsbi knew Dah would pull out an ax-saw even before he saw it.

Every boy in Sanlagita had one. They used them in their lessons, from gutting fish to whittling wood.

But that's not what it would be used for today, if the Pasa brothers had their way.

Dah extended an ax-saw to him.

"Kill it," Dah said.

The tone in his voice had changed, and Hetsbi knew with complete certainty that he would forever be their target, whether he killed the pahaalusk or not.

But he still didn't want to be a coward.

He wanted to take the ax-saw and kill the animal in one swoop, just to show them that he wasn't afraid. That he could do something monstrous if he needed to.

Here's the thing, though: he couldn't.

Could he?

He took Dah's ax-saw, even though he had one of his own. The blade was worn and chipped. Hetsbi never used his ax-saw with confidence, so it still looked brand-new.

The paahalusk blinked up at him. It didn't seem to have any idea what was going on. It opened and closed its mouth. All it cared about was water, probably. Or finding its mother.

"This thing has just been sitting there the whole time," Bio said. "An animal that can't save itself doesn't deserve to live anyway."

"Yes," Dah agreed. "So what are you waiting for, then?"

Had he been waiting for a long time? It didn't seem like it. Their voices sounded far away, and Hetsbi felt like he was far away, too. Like this was something happening between three boys he didn't know.

The handle of the ax-saw slipped, but he didn't drop it. Hetsbi hadn't noticed how much his hands were sweating.

He had to do it. He had no choice. What if he didn't? What then? They already thought he was a hopeless coward. *I can't believe your papa was a sailor. I guess you take after your mama. I hope you know how to work the crops. Ha ha.* They'd said that to him more than once.

If he didn't do this, how much worse would it get?

He tightened his grip.

It's going to die anyway, he thought.

If I do it quickly, it won't even hurt. I'm probably doing it a favor. At least it won't have to suffer.

He would go for the soft, fleshy part of its neck. That was the only way.

He swallowed. Shifted his feet.

One swoop—that's all it would take.

He inhaled deeply.

A little voice screamed in his head: Do it fast or don't do it.

Do it fast.

Do it fast.

Do it fast.

"Hey—what—" Dah blurted out.

At first Hetsbi thought he would comment on the way

Hetsbi was holding the ax-saw, as if he'd held it *like a girl*, or maybe he was talking about the pahaalusk; maybe the pahaalusk had suddenly bared teeth and threatened to attack them all, but when he looked up, he saw that Dah was staring at something, something coming from the mountain, something making the weeds bend this way and that.

It was Lalani.

"Is she coming *out* of the *mountain*?" Bio asked.

She didn't see them. She wobbled, like it pained her to move. Her hair was tangled and stuck out in every direction.

"What was that stupid sahyoon doing in the mountain?" said Dah.

Sahyoon, meaning *round face*.

Sahyoon, meaning *not pretty*.

There was no word for boys who weren't attractive, but for girls it was sahyoon. Every time they called Lalani that, Hetsbi's heart secretly broke for her. But he didn't tell them to stop. He could never find the words, or his voice, to do that.

Bio's eyes narrowed. "We should—"

Another sound. From the opposite direction this time. They froze.

The menyoro was out for a walk.

And they were three schoolboys, standing somewhere they weren't supposed to be. The village rules were strict and simple: after schoolwork, home. Community first. Playing games did not help the community.

Not that this was much of a game.

"Let's go!" Dah said, in a loud whisper. He snatched the ax-saw out of Hetsbi's hand, and he and his brother darted off, moving stealthily so the menyoro wouldn't notice them.

Hetsbi fell on his knees next to the pahaalusk. From this vantage point, he could see tiny bubbles of froth inside the animal's mouth.

"I wouldn't have done it," Hetsbi whispered.

He wouldn't have—right?

Hetsbi and the pahaalusk hid in the weeds together until the menyoro passed them by.

The Strongest Fish

The menyoro cradled the heartbeat of the village in his hand. He was their leader, their healer, the only man on the island who could settle disputes or treat the sick, and this made him very powerful. The menyoro did not marry. The people were his children.

He was not a loving father.

When he arrived at Lalani's house just before she did, she considered it both fortunate and unfortunate.

Fortunate, because no one paid much attention when she walked through the door.

Unfortunate, because she knew right away why he was there.

"Exhausting, going from home to home," the menyoro was saying. He stood between Drum and Kul, looking down at Lalani's mother, who lay on the hard floor with a sheen of sweat across her face. They barely glanced at Lalani. "I hope this isn't the start of another outbreak." He had a clipped way of speaking that distinguished him from the other Sanlagitans. Lalani wondered where he'd learned it. "What would become of you all if I got sick myself, eh? Especially since I still haven't selected my successor."

"There's no need," Drum said. "You're young yet, and healthy."

The fact that Drum treated him with respect was testament to the power of the menyoro. Every man in the village wanted to be his successor, but he'd dragged his feet in choosing one.

"I can see already that she is affected by it," said the menyoro. He tilted his head left, right, then left again.

"No swelling, but her skin is warm and her cheeks flushed."

Lalani stood behind the men without saying a word. She didn't want to draw attention to herself, but she was desperate to go to her mother.

"I heard that some have survived it," said Kul.

"She won't," the menyoro said. "Only the strong ones survive."

The way he said it—so matter-of-fact, as if he were talking about a useless fish or insect—sparked anger in Lalani's chest. She was tired and her mind was muddled. Her thumb throbbed where Ellseth's arrowhead had sliced it. She'd spent hours wandering the mountain, and she was thirsty and hungry and weary. Perhaps that's why her anger lit so quickly and burned like fire.

"My mother *is* strong," Lalani said, before she could stop herself.

The menyoro squinted at her, then raised his eyebrows at Drum.

"Pay no attention to her," said Drum. His thumb tapped, tapped, tapped against his leg. "She's just the daughter."

Lalani imagined herself kicking Drum in the knee. Kul, too. If she were like Ziva, maybe she would. Or maybe she'd just take her mother and hide away on the ship that was set to sail the next morning. Cade's brother Esdel Malay was the captain this time, and Esdel seemed like a reasonable man. The Malays were a good family. Kind, and strong.

Just like her father had been.

Her father, who had never returned.

"How long does my wife have?" Drum asked.

The menyoro shrugged. "It's hard to tell with these things. Weeks, I'd say. Some last longer than others. It's like our Sanlagitan fish—one may spoil right away; another may be good to eat for days to come."

Lalani inhaled deeply.

They had compared her mother to a fish.

Lalani's mother fell asleep on her back. Sweat snaked down her forehead. Heat radiated from her skin so feverishly that it warmed Lalani's skin as she nestled close. The men snored across the room. But Lalani could not sleep.

"If you were a fish, you would be mighty," Lalani whispered. "You would survive forever because no one would see you coming."

Lalani rested her temple on her mother's shoulder. *At least she's not awake and in pain*, Lalani thought, though she desperately wanted to hear her mother's voice. She wanted to hear her say it would be okay. She wanted to ask questions about all those mothers and their stories.

Instead, she only heard the raspy whistles of her mother's labored breathing.

"The fishermen would think you were just an average fish, so they would try to catch something bigger or brighter. But if they were to catch you, they would find out how strong you were," Lalani continued. "They would try to cut you open, but you would bite their hands off and go right back into the water."

She paused. She wanted to tell her mother a story. Something to lift her spirits, if only as she slept. The one about the binty—something to remind her of her own mother and times long ago, when she was just a girl—but she'd never had a chance to ask Mora Pasa about it.

The only story she could think of was the one she had just lived. My-Shek. Ellseth. The mountain. The beast. A prick of her thumb, the promise of rain, a small bit of magic. If her mother knew such things could happen, she might believe that anything was possible, including her own survival.

"Mama . . ." Lalani began. *She's asleep,* she thought. *What could it hurt?* "I want to tell you something."

Her mother's breath rattled.

Her fever burned.

Lalani closed her eyes. The words sat on her tongue,

every one of them, every detail, even the breeze from the old tree. But she had made a promise. She had given her word. She swallowed the story away and, without a taller tale to tell, she soon fell asleep.

Sailing Day

When the rising sun slanted into the room the next day, Lalani opened her eyes, expecting to hear rain. But there was only Drum, who kicked her pillow and told her to get up.

"It's Sailing Day," he said.

Lalani turned toward her mother. The blanket was soaked through, but she was still sleeping peacefully.

"Hurry," Drum ordered. "You can see to your mother when we get back."

Lalani, Drum, Kul, and the other villagers advanced together like a great herd to the northern shore. Lalani scanned the crowd for Veyda and broke away as soon as she spotted her.

Lo Yuzi was holding Veyda's hand, which Lalani knew Veyda hated. Hetsbi walked with them, too. Lalani fell in step.

"Where's your mama?" Lo Yuzi said, craning her neck over the crowd.

"The menyoro saw her last night," Lalani replied. "She's sick."

She didn't need to say anything else.

"I'm sorry," Lo Yuzi said. She briefly placed her hand on Lalani's back.

Veyda hurried to Lalani's side.

"I'm sorry, too," she whispered.

The mood was solemn, even though Sailing Days were supposed to be celebratory. It took years to build ships and train sailors, so Sailing Days did not come around often. When they did, the mood was meant to be triumphant.

"Could he do anything for her?" Veyda asked.

But they both knew the answer to that, so they walked in silence the rest of the way.

The villagers reached the northern shore. Danila, Caralita, and Yari—three of Sanlagita's best washerwomen—clutched the hands of their small children. Lalani knew what the washerwomen's hands felt like. Rough, like grains of sand under the skin. Dry and cracked. Swollen knuckles from scrubbing the washerboards for hours. Lalani glanced down at her own hands and wondered what they'd look like when she was older. Maybe they'd be like Lo Yuzi's—dusted with earth.

Lalani and Veyda watched the shipbuilders pull the sailing vessel from its cradle, heaving it behind them with thick ropes. Lined, elderly faces gazed off, expressionless and unexpectant, as if this were yet another chore in a long workday. All the ships looked the same. Large, but not imposing. Designed to carry three men, food, and supplies.

Lalani thought of Ellseth.

I've not seen your island—of course, I haven't—but mine? Isa? It is lush and alive.

"Do you think they'll make it?" Hetsbi asked, bringing Lalani back to the present.

She looked into the sky.

Would it rain?

"No," said Veyda. "I think they'll be dead by noon."

Lo Yuzi made a sound with her tongue—*tsk-tsk*—to scold her daughter for her bluntness.

Every sailor who sailed into the Veiled Sea believed he was different. His ship would be victorious. He would be the first to return, hands full of gold, belly full of exotic fruit, and skin bronzed from the sun. There had once been rumors that all the men had survived and established new villages and hadn't come back so they could keep the fortunes for themselves.

But Ziva changed all that.

She'd hidden herself on a boat bound for Isa, desperate to escape the hardships of her life. Three men were on board, unaware of their stowaway. Three days later the boat reappeared out of the mist—that's how the stories had it, at least. Only one man was left on board. He wasn't wearing any clothes. His chest was raked with fingernail scratches and caked with seawater and vomit. He bumbled out, eyes crazed, and said they'd gotten lost as soon as the ship left Sanlagita. When Ziva had appeared, they thought it was her fault. They believed she had cast a spell on them. *Something*. It *had* to be her fault. They were skilled sailors. Intelligent, brawny, and brave. She was a girl. What other explanation was there?

Ziva had lived on Sanlagita all her life, but none of them had recognized her at first. The ocean had confused them. Muddied their thoughts. They threw her overboard and she fell into the misty water, screaming. Her long hair caught on a plank somehow, tethering her to the ship, so one of the men unsheathed his ax-saw and hacked her hair off. She floated away. The men expected the skies to clear. Their witch was gone.

But things did not get better.

Quite the opposite.

The men forgot where they were or why they were on the water. One sailor jumped off the boat, muttering nonsense. Another followed. The one remaining huddled in the bow and wept until the ship drifted back to the northern shore of Sanlagita. The sailor told his story, then threw up. Eleven crabs crawled from his mouth. He said the sea was unpassable. Seconds later he dropped dead.

For years there were no Sailing Days. But Sanlagita has a short memory, and soon a new generation rose up to undertake the challenge. New sailors announced themselves even as pieces of wreckage from past years drifted onto the beach. These sailors claimed they were stronger and smarter. They never thought they'd be chewed up, too.

This morning, at early dawn, it was Cade's brother Esdel and his two cousins who were ready to sail.

The menyoro stood with his back to the ship and sailors.

"As we all know, it is a great honor to be selected as a sailor. A great honor indeed," he said. "I know this occasion may be difficult for you. I know we have struggled together. We have lost many men to the sea—

many brave and skilled men. But we are Sanlagitans, and this means that we will not bow to defeat. Across this sea is a vast wonderland beyond our imaginings. Legend tells us so. And we will not rest until we have conquered it, with the power and force of Kahna behind us."

He pumped his fists into the air, and the people cheered, although their faces remained solemn.

Lalani thought again of Ellseth. She pressed her thumb to her forefinger to make sure the wound was really there and she hadn't imagined it.

The sky remained cloudless.

Veyda leaned over. Her hair tickled Lalani.

"See how he stands on that platform?" Veyda whispered. "It's only to make him appear taller. That way it seems as if he's more powerful than us. But he's not."

Lalani put her fingers to her lips. What if someone overheard?

"I am confident that Esdel and his men are immune to the water's tricks," the menyoro continued.

"I wonder what the menyoro said when our papas

sailed," Veyda whispered. They'd talked about that many times before, the two of them. "Oh, look—here's Cade."

Yes, Cade was walking up to them. He stood next to Lalani. Veyda often joked that Cade admired Lalani, but Lalani knew better. Cade was the strongest and most handsome boy in the village, and she . . . well, she was a sahyoon. She knew that.

Hetsbi turned to him. "Your brother looks very strong, Cade."

Cade didn't blink. Eyes forward.

The sail flapped in the wind.

"We know you've been disappointed in the past by weaker men," the menyoro continued, conviction in his voice. "But these sailors will not let us down."

Weaker men? The fire in Lalani's chest sparked.

Esdel and his cousins cast off, releasing their ship from the dock. Sailing Days were meant to be momentous, but the villagers were subdued. They all watched the ship disappear into the mist. There was barely a sound.

When the ship was out of sight, the menyoro turned to them again. His face was coated in sweat.

"While we wait for news, I will retire home and send thoughts of hope across the sea. I will say my benedictions as always," he said. "I encourage you to do the same. Take rest today. Back to it tomorrow."

No one moved until he stepped down off his makeshift platform. Then they followed, murmuring quietly. All but Cade.

Lalani, Veyda, and Hetsbi didn't leave right away, either. Neither did Lo Yuzi. It didn't seem right while Cade was still standing there, staring at the sea.

"Things will never change if everyone's asleep," Cade said.

He turned on his heel and went to find his mother.

Pshah on That

Lalani stayed at the Yuzis' house until the sun slipped behind Mount Kahna. Truth be told, she would have liked to spend the night, but she couldn't. Not while her mother was sick. She would have liked to have Veyda stay at her house, too—but Kul made Veyda uncomfortable. Veyda was beautiful, and it hadn't escaped Kul's glowering attention.

Veyda offered to walk her home. Once they were on their way, she nudged Lalani with her elbow and said, "You have a secret, don't you? I can tell."

Lalani pressed her thumb against her forefinger and

glanced at the cloudless sky. Oh, how desperately she wanted to tell her best friend about Ellseth! But she didn't dare. Who knew what would happen?

"I don't have a secret," said Lalani. Her voice wavered. She was a terrible liar.

"Yes, you do," Veyda replied. "But if you don't want to tell your very best friend . . ." She shrugged and grinned.

The water pump came into view. Cade's older brother Agapito was no longer guarding it. Perhaps he and Cade were comforting their mother, who was no doubt crying into her blankets.

"Why are you frowning?" Veyda asked.

"I was thinking about Cade's mother."

Now Veyda frowned, too. "I wish we could bring her a basket of fruit, but we can't afford to share a bite. None of my mother's seedlings is growing at all."

Lalani was relieved that Veyda's attention had shifted away from her secret, even if the subject was grim.

"We should visit anyway, just to give her good wishes," Lalani said.

Veyda's sneaky smile returned. She bumped Lalani with her hip. "*And* so you can see Cade, right?"

"No!" Lalani said, blushing. "I told you, he doesn't look at me that way."

"What makes you think that?"

"No one sees me that way." Lalani lowered her voice and watched her sandals walk along the dirt. "I know what I am."

"Kind and loyal?"

"No," Lalani said. "I'm a sahyoon."

Veyda waved her hand in the air, as if she were snatching up the word and throwing it away.

"Pshah!" she said. "Pshah on that!"

One, Two, One, Two

Lalani counted her mother's breaths. They'd slept so closely all these years, and her breathing was always the same night after night. Inhale, exhale, inhale, exhale, one, two, one, two. When Lalani was younger and had nightmares of her father drowning in the Veiled Sea, her mother's breaths put her to sleep. There had been times, too, when she knew her mother was only pretending to sleep.

Tonight, things were different.

Her mother was asleep, but her breathing was unsteady.

The inhales were ragged. The exhales wheezed. Her

chest ballooned. And the way she kept turning her head, with her chin dipped near her collarbone, scared Lalani more than anything.

More than the eyeless man she'd wagered with.

More than being lost on Mount Kahna.

More than the thought of My-Shek wandering alone.

This was the sound of sickness. Her mother's sickness, racing through her blood.

Her mother could be cold and distant, yes.

But she was still her mama.

Where would Lalani be without her? Where would she go? The thought of staying with Drum and Kul, now snoring from the farthest corner of the room, terrified her. They'd only make her a servant, no doubt. Or worse. If she went anywhere else, she would just be another mouth to feed, and who had resources for that? The menyoro might place her somewhere—but how would that end?

Lalani took her mother's hand. So warm. She kissed her mother's knuckles.

"I'm sorry you're sick, Mama," she whispered.

She brushed a lock of hair from her mother's damp forehead.

She thought of Toppi, the way he'd kicked his feet and beat his fists in the air. How loudly he'd wailed. How much pain was he in? Was her mother in pain now? How much did it hurt?

Lalani closed her eyes, said her benediction silently—*Spare us another night. Remain quiet and peaceful in our gratitude*—then opened them again.

"You have to think good thoughts," she whispered. "To help your spirit get better. Think of Papa."

Lalani thought of him now, too. She didn't remember much. Only pieces. The way his hands felt when he lifted her in the air. The shape of his eyebrows. The wideness of his feet. Surely, he hadn't been perfect. But that was the wonderful thing about memories—sometimes only the good ones stayed put.

Her mother sputtered and coughed. Lalani wiped her chin.

"Daughter." Her mother smiled. Faintly. It was strange

at first; she wasn't a woman who often smiled. "I had a dream of you."

Lalani's heart raced, though she wasn't sure why. Maybe because her mother didn't often speak to her directly any longer, except to delegate tasks. Maybe because her voice sounded strange and distant, as if it belonged to another woman in another time.

"It was a waking dream," her mother continued. "All mothers have the same one. Some forget they have it. Others never forget. I never forgot." She took a breath, blinked. "Do you know what the dream was?"

"No, Mama."

"That things would be better for you." Another breath. "If we want our world to change, we can't keep walking in circles. Can we?"

Lalani's mind swam.

Things will never change if everyone's asleep.

"I don't know, Mama," Lalani said.

Her mother coughed and coughed. Lalani's chest hurt just listening.

"When I don't feel well, I like to think of stories," Lalani continued. "My favorite story is the one about Ziva. But sometimes I change the ending. Instead of drowning in the Veiled Sea, she makes it all the way to Isa."

"You've always been fond of stories," her mother said, closing her eyes.

Lalani wiped her chin again.

"I had a dream of you, too, Mama," Lalani said. "You were the strongest fish in the sea, and you lived forever."

But Lalani's mother had already fallen asleep.

Thank You, Ellseth

At first Lalani thought the sound was part of her dream.

Pit-pat. Pit-pat. Pit-pat.

She didn't open her eyes right away. She was in that blurry space between wakefulness and dreaming, not sure what was real and what wasn't. But the sound continued, growing more determined with each second, as if it was trying to wake her up.

Pit-PAT. Pit-PAT. Pit-PAT.

She opened one eye, then the other. The sounds of her sleeping family faded, and she heard only *pit-PAT! pit-PAT! pit-PAT!*

She bolted upright. The rag she'd been using to wipe her mother's face fell off her chest. She froze. Didn't want to scare the sound away. Because it sounded like—

"Rain."

The word lodged in her throat and barely crawled out of her mouth. So she tried again.

"Rain."

PIT-PAT! PIT-PAT! PIT-PAT! PIT-PAT! Still, no one stirred.

"Rain!"

PITPATPITPATPITPATPITPATPITPATPITPAT PITPATPITPAT

Soon it was just a great swoosh, a tremendous blanket, a shower of hope. Soon it was so loud that Drum woke up. Then Kul. The three of them exchanged glances in the dark, disbelieving.

"Rain," Lalani said again. "Rain!"

She clutched her mother's feverish hand and squeezed, hoping she too would wake up and see the miracle.

"I don't believe it," Drum said.

Lalani closed her eyes. Under her breath so no one could hear, she whispered, "Thank you, Ellseth. Thank you."

The words disappeared.

She would never utter them again.

Rain

It rained for hours. No one left their houses. They sat inside and listened. They watched the rain make mud from the dirt. They put bowls on the floor to catch the drops that squeezed through the slats of wood.

They lost track of time because the sky stayed gray all day. Gray, then black. It kept raining while they slept. When they opened their eyes, the bowls on the floor were full, and still the rain fell.

Hours turned to days.

There wasn't time to celebrate the rain, because it didn't give the earth a moment to drink. It just kept falling. People finally went outside because they couldn't stay indoors forever. They held igugi leaves over their heads, but it didn't matter—they still got wet.

Lalani, soaked to the bone, ran to Veyda's house.

"Will all this rain help the plants grow?" Lalani asked, her heart pounding.

"If it ever stops," answered Veyda.

"What if doesn't?"

"We'll have a flood, sola. That's what."

The girls and Hetsbi spread a handful of pebbles on the floor and played games. How many pebbles can you steal? How many can you pick up at once? Can you guess which bowl it's hiding under?

The rain roared.

When Lalani went home, she tended to her mother. Wiped her forehead. Kissed her cheek. Told her stories— some from Lo Yuzi, some from Mora Pasa, some from herself. An ache beat in her chest. She thought of floods and rising water, and she imagined herself standing in the middle of it all, asking for forgiveness.

* * *

Days became weeks.

The Sanlagitans had never experienced anything like this. Before the drought, there had always been two distinct seasons: rainy and dry. But this dry season had stretched on and on. It was never-ending. Now the rainy season had come—but as a curse, not a gift. Long-forgotten streams swelled into rivers. Dry pockets in the earth became miniature lakes. When people ventured outside, the puddles reached their ankles.

The menyoro sounded his horn—a loud and obnoxious instrument carved from an old pahaalusk shell—but no one could hear it over the rain, so he sent Agapito from door to door to call a village meeting. Everyone gathered, shoulders hunched against the downpour, and moved together through the sludge and mud. Sounds buzzed in Lalani's ears—falling water, splashing sandals, raised voices. Her mother was too sick to do anything but sleep, so Lalani lagged behind Drum and Kul as they joined the mass exodus to the menyoro's house. She found Hetsbi and Veyda. Cade was nearby, too. The rain didn't seem to faze him.

"How is Toppi?" Lalani asked Veyda. She craned her neck, searching for his family.

"About the same, I think. But I haven't gone over in two days," said Veyda. She blinked her dark eyes at Lalani. "How's your mama?"

"About the same."

Veyda grabbed her hand and squeezed it.

The menyoro stood atop the detached shell that once belonged to a full-grown pahaalusk. He raised his arms, palms out, just as he'd done on Sailing Day.

"I sense great panic," he said, speaking loudly. "And I want to reassure all of you that I'm doing all I can to commune with Mount Kahna to determine if there is something we can do to appease the sky. It's clear we are being punished. It could be Ziva's trickery, but I believe it is vengeance from the mountain. Ziva could not be strong enough to control the sun and the rain." He paused. Scanned the crowd with darkened brows. No one made a sound as they stood under the drumbeat of the rain. "Have you all been saying your benedictions?"

The villagers murmured. They exchanged glances, mumbled yes, raised their eyebrows.

This time, Lalani squeezed Veyda's hand. Hetsbi glanced at his older sister, then chewed his bottom lip.

"I understand if you don't want to come forward," the menyoro continued. "But know this. If you haven't said your benedictions, you have brought a great curse upon us, and that curse will only worsen." He lifted his chin. "If you know of someone in this village who does not say them with reverence, reveal that person now."

More murmurs. Louder this time.

After several seconds, the menyoro nodded, as if this was what he'd expected.

"If you reveal those in our community who have wronged our village, you will be rewarded with double rations," he said.

Lalani felt her feet sinking in the mud. She blinked, momentarily blinded by the water in her eyes. No one said anything, but the menyoro was patient. He stood tall and still, as if it wasn't raining at all.

And finally, someone spoke.

"Lalani Sarita did this to us!"

It was Bio Pasa, with his finger pointed directly at her. People moved out of the way, creating a path between accuser and accused.

His brother, Dah, appeared beside him. "Yes! It was Lalani!"

Lalani had the sudden urge to run—fast like a wallecta, quick like a fish. She wanted to climb the tallest tree. Dig a hole in the ground. Heat shot through her body. The fire of shame, embarrassment, fear.

"I—" she began. Her throat had swollen shut.

Someone jostled through the crowd and stepped into the path of Bio's raised finger.

Drum. He leveled his eyes at her. His hand tapped madly against his meaty thigh.

"What's this about?" he asked. The rain matted his hair around his face.

"We saw her!" Bio said, practically frantic. "We saw her come down from the mountain! She was up there!"

"She was! She was!" Dah cried. "Hetsbi Yuzi saw her, too!"

Heads turned to Hetsbi, who took a step behind Veyda. He pursed his lips so tightly that the skin around them turned white.

"What's happening here, boy?" the menyoro asked Bio.

Bio bowed his head quickly in respect. "My brother and I saw Lalani Sarita walking down from Mount Kahna just before the rain started. She looked like she'd been climbing for days."

The menyoro's eyes shifted from Bio to Lalani.

Veyda's hand squeezed her shoulder.

"Is this true?" the menyoro asked.

Lalani pressed her index finger against her thumb, remembering her sworn oath to Ellseth. She'd given her blood for that promise.

"Yes," said Lalani. Rain dripped from her nose.

"What were you doing on the mountain?" the menyoro asked. "You know Kahna is vengeful."

"Yes," Lalani repeated. "But—"

Her voice scurried away.

"But what, girl?" the menyoro said.

"I was trying to catch a shek that got loose."

Bosalene Pasa, Bio and Dah's mother, broke through the crowd. "She lies!" Bosalene yelled. "I haven't lost any shek! None of my shek gets loose!"

Of course she wouldn't admit it. The menyoro docked rations when people didn't tend to their responsibilities properly.

"It was my fault, probably," Lalani continued, more quietly than she intended. "I tried to fix the fence, but it didn't hold."

"Speak up, girl!" the menyoro ordered.

Speak up, girl! Speak up!

Lalani did her best to raise her voice. "A shek got loose and went into the mountain! I tried to catch it, and I got lost!"

"Lies!" someone yelled—she didn't know who. "She angered Kahna, and now we're paying the price!"

Veyda dropped her arm from Lalani's shoulder and took a step in front of her.

"She didn't do anything!" Veyda yelled. "She was just trying to help!"

"Lots of good that's done for us!" Bosalene said. "She should be punished!"

Lalani's heart raced. She felt like she was made of leaves—trembling, vulnerable, falling. People she'd known her whole life were in the crowd—Danila Morendo and all her children, whom Lalani once looked after; the washerwomen that she waved to in the mornings; Maddux Oragleo and his daughters; Cade and his family—but now they'd become one big indistinguishable mob, and she couldn't tell who was saying what. All she heard was the thunderous cry as the village turned against her: "Yes! She should be punished! Punish her!"

The menyoro raised his hands, and the villagers' cries quickly settled down.

"All of us must increase our benedictions. Repeat them for hours if need be," the menyoro said. Then he cast his eyes to Drum. "This girl lives under your care, does she not?"

"Yes, menyoro," Drum replied.

"Are you afraid to subjugate your household?"

The muscles in Drum's jaw clenched. His cheeks flushed red. "I am afraid of nothing, menyoro," he said.

"Teach her a lesson, then," the menyoro said.

A Lesson

Drum clutched Lalani's arm and she was forced to walk beside him on the way home, taking two steps for one of his, with Kul striding behind them. Just before Lalani and her uncle reached the door, Cade hurried their way, his ax-saw hitting his thigh, water splashing around his ankles. Drum and Kul stopped and waited for him to speak.

"What is it, boy?" Drum finally said.

Cade's eyes moved from Lalani to Drum and back again.

"I was just—" He paused, shifting from foot to foot.

Cade was known for being sure of himself. But Drum and Kul had a way of inciting fear, and when they stood together, they resembled a fortress.

"Speak, boy!" Kul said.

"My mother hasn't been well since my brother sailed," said Cade. He cleared his throat. "Perhaps Lalani could work in our house as her punishment for—"

"What kind of punishment is that?" Drum said. He turned toward the door and pushed it open with one hand, still holding Lalani with the other. "Besides, she has her own sick mother to look after. Go away."

Cade stumbled back and nodded. He ran his hand over his rain-soaked hair. Lalani had seen him do this before when he was focused on a task. It was one of his tells. And she knew now that his task had been to save her from whatever punishment Drum had waiting, because they both suspected it would be terrible.

When the door closed between them, Lalani had never felt more alone.

"Find a washerwoman and bring me a basin," Drum barked to Kul, who ran back into the rain.

Lalani stood in the center of the room. She wanted to run to her mother, curl up close, listen to her breathing, feel her skin, even if one was labored and the other fevered. She clasped her hands in front of her. Stay very still, she told herself. Show no fear.

"Stupid girl," Drum said over and over again. "Stupid, stupid girl."

What would he do with the basin? There was no way to know.

Stay very still.

Show no fear.

Kul returned shortly with a sparkle of anticipation in his eye. He placed the basin between his father and Lalani.

"Pick it up," Drum said to her.

It required two hands. The mouth of the basin was wide, but Lalani lifted it without trouble.

"Follow me," he said.

She did. Kul did, too. Lalani hoped to see Cade

lingering outside, but he was gone. She and Kul followed Drum through the rain, through the splashing puddles, through the storm, directly to the water pump in the center of the village.

"Stand here," Drum said.

She did.

He slapped the bottoms of both of her elbows. Lift the basin and straighten your arms, the gesture said.

She did. She looked like she was offering it to someone, but there was no one on the receiving side. Just Drum leaning close to her ear—so close that she felt his breath on her skin.

"You think you can make a fool of me? We'll see who is made a fool," he said. "You won't leave this spot until you're given permission. And you won't drop that basin."

Drum ordered Kul to stay and keep an eye on her. Once Drum was out of sight, Kul gathered a bundle of igugi leaves and tied them to the pump so he could sit under their protection.

"Let's see how long those arms last," he said.

* * *

Don't be fooled by an empty basin. It doesn't weigh much, but it collects things. Like raindrops. One, two, three, one after the other, *PIT-PAT, PIT-PAT, PIT-PAT.* A basin as wide as this one can hold countless drops of rain, and when the rain was coming down like it was in Sanlagita, you may as well be holding Mount Kahna itself.

Lalani's biceps burned first. The pain wrapped around her narrow muscles and crawled toward her wrists. Her back ached next. Then her legs. When the basin was half-full, her wrists threatened to go numb and she gave away her first tell: her lower lip trembled. She shoved it under her front teeth, but Kul had noticed.

"Don't even *think* about dropping it," he said. "Or you'll really get what's coming."

What could be worse than standing here, in the open, as the villagers glared through cracks in their doors? Some came out of their houses and walked through the sheet of rain to spit on her, or in the basin.

Danila Morendo gathered all her children for that very purpose, even the littlest ones who could barely walk.

"May Kahna curse your soul," she said.

Lalani didn't speak to them.

Stay very still, she told herself.

Show no fear.

Don't drop the basin.

At some point, her arms gave up. It was bound to happen. The basin was incredibly heavy. How long had she been standing there? Hours? It was impossible to tell. Ignoring Kul, she rested the basin on the ground and took a breath. But there wasn't time for many of them. Kul glared at her, and she lifted the weight again.

Drum emerged from the rain, carrying something.

A blood-soaked wallecta on a spear.

He thrust the spear deep into the muddy earth next to her and walked away.

The ground was too soft for the weight of the wallecta. The spear tilted and tilted. Lalani didn't move. Every part of her burned. Even her eyes.

When the wallecta fell, she did, too. She hit the mud one second after the basin, which overturned and emptied everywhere—on her, the dead wallecta, and the spear. She saw Kul's boots come toward her, splashing dirty water in her face.

She thought he was going to kick her.

He laughed instead.

Then he walked away.

She closed her eyes. I'll be fine here, she told herself. If I never get up, I won't have to face anyone again.

She stayed there until someone—Cade?—picked her up and carried her home.

Straightening Out

"Whatever the punishment was, it wasn't enough," Dah Pasa said as he impaled a small fish on his fishing hook. The boys were sitting on blocks outside the schoolhouse, perfecting their baiting skills. They were under a wooden lean-to, but drops of rain still splashed them and their faces were wet.

Dah's brother Bio nodded, eyes on his own task.

"If she wants to go to the mountain alone, they should just let her and leave her there," said Bio.

Cade and Hetsbi were nearby. Hetsbi's hook still wasn't baited. Cade's was, and he leaned forward, elbows on his knees, eyeing the brothers.

"She's lucky she didn't get killed. She should thank her father and the menyoro," Dah continued. "Stupid sahyoon."

Hetsbi tried not to look at the Pasa brothers, but he couldn't help himself.

"What's the matter?" said Dah. "Don't want us talking about your girlfriend? You like that sahyoon or something?"

The Pasa brothers laughed.

Bio wiped the rain from his forehead with the back of his hand. "You wanna kiss her moon face?"

Hetsbi studied his hook.

"You know whose face I'd like to kiss?" Dah said, swatting his brother on the knee. "Veyda's." He turned his mouth into an *O*. "Ai-yay."

"Your sister is enough to make me wanna cross two oceans, Hetsbi!" Bio said. "She uses her brain too much, though, so she'd need some straightening out."

"We should race home. Winner gets Veyda," said Dah.

Bio snorted. "And loser gets the sahyoon!"

Dah was roaring with laughter when Cade sprang up like a fish and lunged at Bio, fists ready. One of them landed on Bio's square jaw, the other on his temple, and soon Bio was down, sprawled in the mud, throwing his own confused blows but not landing any, with Cade over him, and then Dah was there, wrapping both arms around Cade's chest and pulling him back. But Cade's anger was forceful—he threw Dah off and Dah went down, too, and now Cade turned on him instead. Dah yelled and kicked while his brother moaned and struggled to stand. It all happened so fast that Hetsbi barely had time to think, but then he *did* think. He thought: *Should I help him? How do I help him? Will I be strong enough? What if I get hit?* And while he was working out the answers to each of those questions, Taiting rushed over.

"What's going on here! What's going on!" Taiting yelled frantically, pulling at Cade's arm. His touch brought Cade back from wherever he'd been and he stood still, all but his chest, which heaved and heaved.

Hetsbi was frozen, his bait in one hand and hook in the other. The other boys, too. They formed a small, curious, and excited semicircle around all the commotion. Hetsbi took in the blood on Dah's lip and the reddening welt across Bio's left cheek.

Cade didn't have a mark on him.

All three boys breathed hard. Parts of their bodies were caked in mud.

"What's going on here?" repeated Taiting.

"He went crazy!" Dah yelled. "We were just sitting here, minding our own business!"

"The menyoro should make him a piler!" said Bio.

Pilers cleaned up the village sewage. They were usually old men who couldn't do anything else, or men "cursed by Kahna with uselessness," as the menyoro put it.

"Calm down, calm down," said Taiting. He motioned for Cade to stand by him, which he did. "Cade, what's the meaning of all this?"

But Cade's mouth had been stitched together. There was fire in his eyes.

Hetsbi bit his bottom lip. Why didn't Cade say anything? Why didn't he tell Taiting what the Pasa brothers had said? Then Taiting would understand—wouldn't he? The punishment might not be as severe, at least.

"Did anyone see what happened?" Taiting asked the other boys.

"He went crazy, that's what happened!" Dah cried, dabbing his busted lip with his fingertips. "He's probably losing his mind because he knows his brother—"

"Enough," Taiting snapped.

Dah exchanged a look with Bio but didn't say anything else.

Taiting turned his attention back to the others.

"Did anyone see anything?" he repeated.

The hook and bait in Hetsbi's hands were the heaviest items on earth. Cade was looking at him. There was nothing in his eyes that said *speak up for me* or *why aren't you talking?* but words formed in the back of Hetsbi's mouth nonetheless.

Dah and Bio were saying terrible things about Lalani and my sister.

Dah and Bio were being disrespectful.

Dah and Bio are cruel.

Dah and Bio tried to make me kill a pahaalusk.

Dah and Bio have tormented me for as long as I can remember.

I'm happy Cade did it.

I wish I could have done it.

The words gathered and readied themselves to march into the world. All they needed was Hetsbi's permission. But he waited too long to give it, and before he could, Taiting disappeared into the schoolhouse with Cade and the Pasa brothers.

Again

Mud. Everywhere. Caked on Lalani's legs. Nestled in the folds of her elbows and knees. Turning her hair into a thick nest of earth and twigs. The rain didn't wash it away; it only made more sludge. The worst part? Her fingernails. The muck had buried itself into every crevice, and now her nails were black. But when you're sliding down a wet mountain, trying to find your grip—especially if your body is already weakened—you need something to burrow into the ground. Hands and feet are usually your best option.

She was dirty.

She ached.

But she'd made it.

The rain fell.

The land shifted.

But she was here, at Ellseth's. Again.

The door was ajar. When she knocked, it opened. Ellseth was sitting in his chair. The staff—his udyo—nearby. The arrowhead dangled in its pouch around his neck. Everything was as it had been before.

"Ellseth?" said Lalani.

He turned and she shivered. She'd been so determined to get here that she hadn't prepared herself for seeing him again. His missing eyes. Those horns.

"Is that you, Girl?" he replied.

She stepped inside. "Yes."

Maybe it was the rain, which still poured outside. Maybe it was the weight of everything that had happened. But the air felt different in here now.

Lalani sat in the same place as before. There were no jarred bulb flies to add any light. The mud was so thick on her body, it was as if she was wearing an additional layer of skin.

"I need your help." She cleared her throat. "You were incredibly kind to grant me a wish. If it's not too much to ask, I hoped you'd grant me another." The mud split and cracked around her mouth as she spoke.

Ellseth rested both hands atop his staff and lowered his chin.

"Is that so?" he said.

Lalani nodded, then remembered he couldn't see her. "Yes," she said. "If it's not too much to ask."

"Actually, it's quite a lot to ask." He lifted his hand in the air and snapped his fingers. "I made rain for you. And now you are greedy enough to ask for something more?"

She wished Veyda were with her. Anyone, really. She didn't want to do this on her own. But she'd started this whole thing, hadn't she?

"I'm sorry," she said. A twinge of fear pinched at her heart. "I appreciate what you've done. And I see now that I should have spoken more clearly last time. I asked for rain, and you provided rain. But I never said how much or for how long. It's my fault, I know."

Was it, though? Nagging thoughts whispered in the back of her mind: *Surely he knew what you meant. Even without eyes, he knew what he was doing. Look how old he is. Look at his white hair. He's lived long enough to know that you didn't want him to flood the island. Why should you apologize?*

"It's made things worse for the village," she explained. "I only wanted the plants to grow. I didn't know it would—"

"Oh, you didn't know!" Ellseth said. "How convenient."

Lalani frowned. "I'll never bother you again. I promise."

He tilted his head, as if considering this. "And what do you ask for this time?" When she didn't answer right away, he banged his staff against the floor. "Speak, Girl!"

The sudden movement startled her to her feet.

"I—" she began. "I—"

"I, I, what? What, Girl?"

Ellseth stood. He seemed taller.

Lalani pressed herself against the wall.

"I'll quiet the clouds," he said. He gripped his wooden staff, flipped it upside-down, and tapped the low ceiling. Then he reached for the pouch around his neck. "But last time you gave me three drops of blood—"

The rain stopped.

Just like that.

The silence was immediate, shocking.

"—and you must pay a debt again."

Lalani opened her hand, palm up, and stepped toward him, ready to offer more blood.

"I understand," she said. "I'll put my hand here, on the table."

"You'll put your—" he repeated, surprised and half-mocking. "For what purpose, Girl?"

"So you can cut my thumb."

He laughed. "Your *thumb?* You think I want your thumb?"

"I thought—"

"What need do I have for your *thumb*? I have thumbs. I don't want your *thumb*." He moved toward her. One step, two. He placed a hand on her cheek, like a father comforting his child. "I want your eyes."

Her eyes?

He ran his index fingers over her eyes now. She jumped back, horrified.

"I don't understand," said Lalani, each word trembling in unfamiliar silence.

"I think you do."

It felt like he was looking at her. *Through* her.

But that didn't make any sense, did it?

Lalani glanced around the room.

He couldn't see her.

It would be easy to escape.

She lifted her left foot slowly so as not to make any noise. Then she placed it gently on the ground behind her.

Something shifted beneath her. A hum, almost.

It's your imagination, she told herself. It's your fear.

The right foot next.

Again, the hum.

It came from the earth. As if the ground was groaning.

She'd moved back one full step.

Left foot again.

"If you're trying to escape, it's useless."

Before Lalani could reply—to say what? She didn't know—the hum swelled into a roar, and both she and Ellseth clutched the table to keep from falling. The world was moving.

"Please don't do this," she said. "Please don't wake the mountain."

Lalani imagined her village buried under rock. Her mother. Veyda, Hetsbi, and Lo Yuzi. The animals. My-Shek. Cade. It would all be her fault. Again. The ground shifted with such force that Lalani slammed the side of the table and she fell to one knee. Ellseth's legs splayed out at ridiculous angles as he caught his balance.

"Give me your eyes," he said. "And I'll make it stop."

The growl in his voice—there was something familiar about it.

Kahna roared.

Snap!

The walls were collapsing.

Snap!

Another plank, behind her.

Soon the house would fall on them.

"I'll do it!" Lalani cried. "I'll give you my eyes!"

Ellseth reached out toward her, but when a third board snapped under his feet, he went down, and so did the udyo. Lalani snatched it without thinking and immediately wished for the mountain to go back to sleep, hoping the powers of the magical cane would make everything quiet again. She was answered with *Snap! Snap! Snap!* as the house burst apart around them.

Snap! Snap! Snap!

They were sliding. Kahna was pulling them down. Lalani would have screamed, but all the air had left her body, and then she heard the most terrifying sound of all. A wave of dirt, mud, and branches thundered toward her through the space where Ellseth's door had been. She clutched the udyo, but Kahna was too strong and it slipped out of her grasp and into the deafening slide of earth.

Lalani turned toward Ellseth and caught a glimpse of his contorted face and heard his pathetic and confused cry.

"Help me!" he cried. "Help me, Girl!"

That's when she realized *he'd* been the mountain beast all along, *he'd* been the one who attacked her. She didn't look away, though, not even when the wave of earth gained power and they were part of it, just two more twigs being swept down, down, down, as if they weighed nothing, as if they *were* nothing. She couldn't stand to see his face, or his hands clawing the air, so she reached for him, and now her legs were above her head because she was rolling, rolling, the thunder so loud in her ears that her head rang, but still she searched for him, she wanted to save him, even though he'd wanted her eyes, and finally she felt something—but it wasn't his hand, it was the pouch that he wore around his neck, and she thought *maybe if I hold on to this, I can pull him out of the earth*, and even as the thought crossed her mind she knew it was silly, that it wouldn't be strong enough to hold a man, and she was right. The pouch snapped loose, and suddenly Lalani's mouth was full of wet dirt and leaves and she curled herself into a ball, as tight as she could, with no time to think of anything else except how foolish she was.

Only a Mountain

The Pasa brothers had already broken off from the path when the rain ended. Hetsbi and Cade continued on for some minutes—Cade ahead, as always—but when the clouds suddenly cleared, they both stopped and looked at each other. They were dripping wet. They leaned their heads back and studied the sky. Rain never behaved this way.

Their sandals pushed into the soft mud.

"Strange," said Cade.

The boys continued on and didn't stop again until they heard the distant sound of thunder. They paused and turned toward the sound. It was coming from Kahna.

Cade put his hand on his ax-saw.

"What's that?" he said, more to himself than anyone.

Hetsbi looked at the mountain. It stood mighty and tall, but there was something unusual about it, too.

"It's changing shape," Cade said, suddenly breathless. "It's—"

He was right. The mountain was both changed and unmoving, as if one side of its face was slipping away while the rest of it stayed in place. There was no smoke, just a groan. The ground shook under their feet.

Cade's eyes widened. "Kahna is coming!" he hollered. He gestured at Hetsbi to follow him, then took off at an incredible speed. He yelled to anyone who could hear him as he ran: "Kahna is coming! Kahna is coming!"

Hetsbi ran, too. Not as fast as Cade, but faster than he'd ever run before. Because now he understood what it meant—the terrifying sound and the shifting mountain. His greatest fear was happening. The mountain was hungry and angry and it was coming for them. His heart caught in his throat as he encountered other boys on their way home from school, many of whom had figured out what was going on and were running, too.

Hetsbi thought about his mother and sister.

He thought about how the mountain would feel when it clenched its teeth around them.

Cade ran and screamed—"Kahna is coming! Kahna is coming!"—and others joined him in the warning. The village erupted in panic.

Cade and Hetsbi parted ways as soon as their houses came into view. Hetsbi found Veyda and his mother outside, staring at the sky.

"Kahna is coming!" yelled Hetsbi.

Veyda understood right away and pushed Hetsbi and their mother into the house, to the wall that was farthest away from the mountain. Lo Yuzi told them to curl into balls and hold each other. So they did.

They listened to the screams, wails, cries of fear outside. They felt the earth shake.

Hetsbi saw it all as if it had happened already—the

three of them being pushed by the mountain, trampled by its force, buried forever. A thousand images flashed through his mind—his final thoughts, he assumed—but one picture that kept appearing again and again was that of Cade looking at him after the fight.

I will die a coward, Hetsbi thought.

He closed his eyes.

Buried

Hetsbi did not die that day.

He was not buried by the mountain.

He did not feel its teeth clench around him as he crouched in a corner.

Here's who did:

Ellseth. Bosalene Pasa. Her sons, Dah and Bio. Mora, who'd once known the girl Ziva. My-Shek.

And the menyoro.

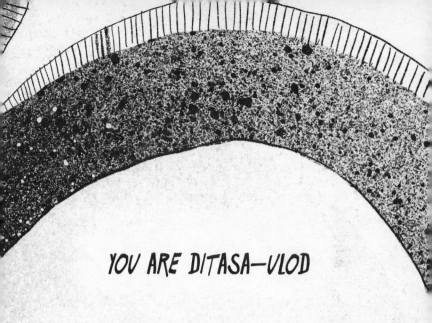

YOU ARE DITASA—VLOD

Imagine you're an exquisite eel. You are slender, long, and perpetually wet, but you never notice because how would you know that you are wet if you are forever in the water? You don't even know what this word means. You only know that your world is water, and water is magical and ever-changing. Land is dry and offensive. You don't understand why anyone would want to live there, but then, we can't always choose where to exist. We come into the world with little say in the matter.

You are thankful to be a water creature. Here,

you are among your people: the maidensharks—with their sharp back fins, scaled green tails, and beautiful cascading hair—who could have been your enemy, if you were a jealous person. And the cantabrito, the sly water spirits who look like vines. Not much frightens you, but the way the cantabrito climb and entangle something just before they devour it can be unsettling—even though they are at your mercy and never act without your bidding. Evil though they are, the cantabrito are your people, too. As are the uga, ilma, and shuzi. You rule them all.

You are Ditasa-Ulod. The water is your kingdom. Your body is a miraculous ribbon with the head of a beautiful woman. Your skin sparkles like the northern stars. Your eyes shine and reflect the water. Your lips are a light shade of blue, and there are gills behind your ears, so you can breathe when you swim. Your hair is an unusual shade of yellow—almost white—and it's long, brittle, and unruly.

There are creatures here whose souls are as black

as the ocean floor, but you are not one of them. You have a kind spirit, but you can be vexed. Certainly you can. Have you killed? Yes. Do you regret it? No. Because it was always to protect your creatures. Your cantabrito. Your maidensharks. Your uga, ilma, and shuzi.

You don't want to drown the outsiders who try to cross your kingdom, but what choice do you have? You can't see inside their hearts. If you could, you would wiggle your way in and swim around. Make sure they are worthy.

But life doesn't work that way.

Yes, the creatures here can be dark.

But at least they aren't humans.

Waste Nothing

Lalani curled into a ball. A loset tree, broken from its roots, rushed toward her and reached out, wrapping a cluster of narrow branches around her waist. The tree held tight as they tumbled together. When the earth stopped, their limbs were entangled. The tree was broken, but Lalani was not.

She unwrapped the branches from her waist and legs. She wiggled her toes. She wiggled her fingers and discovered she was still holding Ellseth's pouch. She considered tossing it, but when you're Sanlagitan, you waste nothing. Perhaps Veyda could use the arrowhead. She tied it around her neck.

Lalani wondered, briefly, if she was dead and had entered another realm. The sky overhead was clear and bright blue. But the sounds weren't peaceful. Wailing, screaming. She stood, unsteady legs on unsteady earth. She was still on the mountain, but near the base now.

The world had changed. There were huge mounds of mud where the loomers and the shek should be. A bolt of panic—My-Shek. What had happened to My-Shek? And the menyoro's house? Gone. There were splintered trees and big rocks among the houses in the village. The crops were buried. The flooded plants were now trapped under layers of mud.

Lalani made her way down to the village, slowly.

The past few weeks unfurled in her memory.

She thought: this is all my fault.

She'd only wanted to help.

She'd only wanted to save her mother. Cure Toppi.

She'd only wanted the plants to grow.

How stupid she'd been, to think that she could do those things.

"My uncle is right," she whispered, to herself.

The village would have been better without her. She only made things worse. Look at what she'd done. Her wishes had destroyed everything.

How could she possibly fix this?

She stopped and sat down. Her bottom sank into the earth.

She looked south, where the fishing boats were hurrying back to shore. Then north, to the Veiled Sea.

An idea blossomed. A ridiculous one.

What if she could find that yellow flower and give it to Veyda?

What if she could bring life's fortunes to the village?

What if she ran away, like Ziva?

What if she reached Isa?

Yes, she was a twelve-year-old girl.

Yes, men had died before her.

But—what if, though?

What if?

In the Darkest of Night

The Yuzi home was not destroyed. When the sun set, Veyda, Hetsbi, and their mother were safely wrapped in their blankets. Hetsbi and Lo Yuzi were asleep.

Veyda was not.

Her eyes were wide open. She heard low voices outside but couldn't tell what was being said. Everyone knew now that the Pasa family and the menyoro were gone. Several villagers were injured but would recover. Veyda wished desperately that she could tend to them—*really* tend to them, by setting their bones or wrapping their wounds—but girls weren't meant for such things.

And she had other things on her mind, anyway.

Everyone had been accounted for except Lalani. Drum and Kul had pounded on the door just after sunset, demanding that she come home.

"She's not here," Lo Yuzi had said, turning to Veyda with furrowed brows.

Veyda shook her head in agreement. No. Lalani was not there.

Drum and Kul had refused to take her word for it, of course. They thudded in their heavy boots through the house and checked the rooms. When they finally left, Lo Yuzi and Hetsbi both asked Veyda where Lalani was, and Veyda had to admit that she didn't know.

"What if she went back to the mountain?" Hetsbi's eyes were wide and terrified.

"Quiet," said Lo Yuzi.

"What if she went back to the mountain and the beast got her?" he said.

"Enough!" Lo Yuzi snapped. She rarely snapped at either of them, but it had been a long day, full of destruction and worries, and no one had patience for anything.

She told them to get to bed. Minutes later she joined them, and she and Hetsbi drifted off, exhausted.

But Veyda couldn't sleep.

Where was Lalani? Her sola, her best friend? Horrifying thoughts nudged into her head, no matter how hard she tried to push them away. Lalani, buried by the landslide. Lalani, her heart quiet and still. Her heart made of clouds.

As the hours passed, Veyda convinced herself that Lalani was dead. Her chest and stomach clenched into a knot and she bit her lip to stop herself from sobbing. But the next moment, she was convinced that Lalani was okay—maybe she had gotten lost, and she was home right now, waiting until morning to visit.

Back and forth Veyda's thoughts went.

The truth arrived when she least expected it, when it was the darkest and quietest part of the night.

Lalani appeared in the doorway, like a ghost. At first

Veyda thought it *was* a ghost and her breath caught in her throat. She thought: Lalani died on the mountain, and now her spirit has come to tell me! But she reminded herself that she didn't believe in ghosts.

This was a living, breathing Lalani. She'd never seen Lalani move so purposefully and lightly.

Veyda shot into a sitting position.

"Shh," Lalani said. She tiptoed toward Veyda's blanket and crouched in front of her, whispering. "I can't explain now. But I have to go."

Veyda opened her mouth to speak.

"There's no time for questions," Lalani continued. "I just wanted you to know I was okay, and to ask you for a favor."

"But—where are you going?" Veyda asked. "Are you doing it? Running away, like Ziva? Are you—"

Hetsbi turned over and sighed in his sleep. Lalani lifted her finger to her lips.

"May I ask you a favor, sola?" she whispered.

"Of course," Veyda answered.

"My mother is sick, and she'll only get worse. Ask Drum if you can move her here, to your house, so you and Lo Yuzi can take care of her." Lalani stood up. "Ask Lo Yuzi to tell her stories for me."

"But—"

Before Veyda could say another word, Lalani was gone.

On the Veiled Sea

Lalani picked the first boat she saw at the light of dawn. The one on top of the pile, with streaks of auburn on the hull. She grabbed a paddle and tossed it inside—*plunk*— then dragged the boat toward the shore. It was nonsense, what she was doing. A girl slipping away into the sea in a small scouting boat—who ever heard of such a thing?

When she was close enough to feel the water against her toes, she stopped. The mist was thick. She'd never been to the northern shore alone. She felt so small. A little girl with a little boat. A big, wide ocean with an open mouth.

Her body was sore and the mud, now cracking off, made her skin itch.

She wanted to sleep forever.

But she had to do this.

"Look at all that happened because of you," she said, to no one.

This was the only way to make things right.

And if she never returned—well, the village would have lost nothing. Nothing but a twelve-year-old girl who was as useless as a wallecta.

Once she was on the water, Lalani couldn't tell if the mist was coming up from the waves or down from the sky. It lay across the surface like a blanket, covering everything so completely that the sloshing and rocking of the boat were the only signs that she was floating. It hovered around her. She could barely see her hand in front of her face.

Was she moving or staying in the same place?

She couldn't tell.

She lifted the paddle and pushed the water with it.

Was she making a terrible mistake?

Had she already made one?

She wanted to turn around but didn't. She would concentrate on what was ahead of her, not behind her.

The sound of the water was strange—peaceful, but scary. Every now and then fish made plinking sounds as they leaped in and out of the sea. She couldn't see them, but when you grow up in a fishing village, you come to know their sounds.

That's it, she thought. Think about the fish. Not the mist.

Did fish know the difference between night and day? What was it like to live underwater? Did they know their mothers? Was it better to be a big fish or a little fish? When you're a big fish, all the fishermen want to catch you. Their nets forever nip at your fins. Not a moment's peace. But there are many good things about being big, too. You can eat all the little fish you want, for example. But if you're a little fish, and you're little enough, no one pays any attention. You can hide under a rock, or *plink-plink* out of the water and dive right back down.

No one pays any attention, if you're little enough.

She fought the urge to turn around. There were so many stories about what was ahead. "The north, the north," the villagers said again and again, lost in their daydreams, gathered for Sailing Days, waiting for all of life's fortunes.

One story rose to the surface of Lalani's mind, something Kul had told her years ago.

"I will tell you a secret," he'd said. "None of those stories are true. I know what's really to the north."

Lalani didn't ask what. She'd learned not to ask Kul questions.

"Villages," he said. "Full of cannibals. Do you know what cannibals are? They're people who eat people. They hunt them down with spears and eat whatever and whomever they can find. They don't care what part it is. It's all food to them."

He paused. "That's what happens to the men who

disappear after Sailing Day. They wash up on the shore of a cursed island, and three heartbeats later, there's a spear in their backs and they're strung up over an open fire. Sometimes the cannibals don't even bother with the spear."

The image of men and boys turning on sticks and roasting like hearty vegetables stayed with Lalani for a long time. She tried not to think of her father, but she always did.

Veyda said it was all lies.

"Don't believe him," she said. "He only wants to frighten you. Never trust someone who wields power through fear."

Lalani pushed into the mist and looked over her shoulder, expecting to see Sanlagita. But the world was the same on all sides.

Was she moving or staying still? The boat was hard to steer.

Which way was Sanlagita?

The mist had a strange effect. Like something was slipping away. Like someone had placed a piece of thread across her hand and now they were pulling it between her fingers.

What was it?

She looked at her feet. Maybe she'd lost something in the boat. But what? All she had was this object around her neck. Wait—what was this thing, anyway?

Arrowhead.

The word sprung out of nowhere.

Arrowhead?

Why would she have it around her neck?

She then realized she had her hand clasped around a long piece of wood and the wood was inside the mist.

What was this?

Paddle.

But her boat was so small. Why would she take things she didn't need?

Paddle.

What an odd word. Both familiar and meaningless.

She studied *Paddle*. What was it for?

The thread slipped between her fingers. She wanted to pull it back. She needed to think clearly. A rational thought in the corner of her brain told her the thread was her mind.

She was losing her mind.

No, that can't be.

Her mind wasn't made of thread. Besides, she was too young to lose her mind.

Wait—how old was she, anyway?

A number did not occur to her.

She listened, hoping someone would whisper it to her.

Twelve.

Yes, she remembered now. She was twelve.

"I will say my name aloud," she said into the mist. "And I'll repeat it again and again and again so I don't lose my mind."

She straightened her back.

Pay attention.

She had to say her name. She had to keep her bearings. She had to remember her purpose.

She was escaping something. Trying to make it right. Wasn't she?

A terrible wrong had happened.

"My name is Lalani Sarita," she said. She closed her eyes and breathed deeply. "My name is Lalani Sarita. My name is Lalani Sarita. My name is Lalani Sarita. My name is . . ."

Letters and sounds dripped from her tongue.

Water licked the boat. Otherwise, it was silent. She clutched the pouch around her neck and tried desperately to remember what her purpose was. She had the distinct feeling that she was escaping, but she also sensed that she wasn't escaping at all—she was searching. Or maybe she was doing both?

The mist was strange and alive and it toyed with her brain.

Then: a noise. Faint, but there. She flinched and steered in the direction it was coming from, but she couldn't see the opposite end of the boat, much less the source of an indistinct sound from far away.

Wait. It was closer now.

Splashing. Gentle, but determined.

She squeezed the paddle, wondering if she could use it as a weapon.

The little boat tilted suddenly, and she tried to scream, but it came out as a short, strangled shriek.

The vessel righted itself.

Was it gone? Was it a man who wanted to roast her over an open fire?

Where had she gotten such an idea?

She scrambled around the little boat on her knees, peering over the side. The sound had returned, but it was less determined now.

The wood of the boat dug into her knees.

The mist was so thick.

She scooted back as far as she could, which wasn't far at all.

It was quiet again, but something was there. The

tempo of the water had changed. There were sounds of subtle movement—gurgles and splashes. She imagined a beast on its haunches, and here she was, easy prey.

Perhaps I should jump overboard, she thought.

But what good would that do?

She brought her knees to her chest and waited for something to spring from the water.

I will be swallowed whole like a little fish, she thought. And I can't even remember my name.

Soft sounds are loud when the world is silent. The gentle splashing of water becomes a tidal wave. That's what Lalani heard as she sat there with her heart pounding. A hungry, angry wave. She knew she was on water and she knew she was alone, but she could not remember why or how. She did know this, however: the mist around her had lifted, and now she saw what it meant to be alone, here, at this moment.

Water. Everywhere. Endless. And she was small— this, she also knew—and so was her boat, and so was the splashing just a few feet away. The water plinked upward like a tiny crested wave. Lalani didn't want to look, but she could look at nothing else.

Splish. Plink. Splish. Plink.

The wave moved closer.

Splish. Plink. Splish. Plink.

The water rippled like a stone had just been tossed there, but of course it hadn't.

The boat swayed.

Lalani didn't move.

Something was underneath her.

Splish.

Plink.

Splish.

Plink.

The boat tilted, forcing Lalani to unclench her hands and hold tight to the sides.

"Go!" she said weakly. A pebble hitting a boulder.

The boat stilled, then lifted and lurched.

"Go!"

What would happen if she fell into the water? Did she know how to swim? She couldn't remember.

Lurch.

"Stop!" Not demanding. Pleading.

Suddenly, without warning, a pair of eyes broke the surface of the water.

Now, the head.

And—what was this?

A shell.

And webbed feet, paddling frantically.

She knew what this was, didn't she? Her mind clambered for the word. It was within reach, so close she could touch it.

Pahaalusk.

Ah, there it was.

Pahaalusk.

This did nothing to soothe her, because she couldn't recall if pahaalusk were dangerous. Did pahaalusk have sharp teeth that would sink into her flesh? Did pahaalusk have claws that could mangle her?

The pahaalusk paddled desperately.

Paddle.

Oh, yes—she had Paddle.

She grabbed it with both hands. Wrapped and unwrapped her fingers.

"Go!" she said. More resolve now that she had a weapon. "Go!"

The pahaalusk coughed. Water spilled from its mouth. Lalani didn't see any teeth, but she still wielded Paddle and yelled, "Go! Go! Go!"

She wished the other girl was there. The smart girl with dark hair. Who was she?

Sola.

Paddle felt heavy. The pahaalusk was drowning, she realized as the boat rocked back and forth, back and forth, taking on water and making her stomach churn.

The creature choked and set its eyes on the safety of the boat. Lalani half stood, determined to make herself as tall and frightening as possible without going over.

A whisper drifted from the mist.

Kill it before it kills you.

Lalani braced herself to swing, but in the next moment the pahaalusk managed to leap into the boat, water pouring from its nostrils, eyes dull but shining, head low and heavy. The boat rocked, both of them now standing in two inches of water, her on one side and the pahaalusk directly opposite.

Lalani stumbled. Raised Paddle.

The boat righted itself, and Lalani was able to stand without trouble, feet wide for balance, knees slightly bent. She swung back, surprised by how difficult it was to lift Paddle, and let out a loud cry—where it came from, she didn't know—as she crashed the weapon against the animal's shell, which had already begun to dry.

Lalani only managed to strike the pahaalusk twice before Paddle cracked and a thin sliver of wood wedged itself into the soft flesh near her thumb. She howled as the paddle clattered to her feet. She shoved her hand into her mouth and sucked on it, hoping to relieve the pain, which was potent enough to make her forget that she was under attack.

The pahaalusk watched her. The paddle had left a crevice in its shell. Its eyes were telling Lalani something important, but she didn't know what.

The whisper again:

You owe it nothing. It's just a pahaalusk. It's nothing like you. You share nothing.

Her thumb throbbed.

She no longer had a worthy weapon, but she had two arms. How easy it would be to slip her skinny arms beneath its slick belly and heave it overboard.

Why not do it?

She moved forward slowly. The mist, thickening again, circled them. She didn't want to startle the pahaalusk, but she needed to move quickly, and she did.

Its belly was softer than she imagined. It shifted its webbed feet to make room for her arms.

She'd thought this would be simple, but she had underestimated the pahaalusk's weight. She tried to flip it overboard but stumbled back with both arms still around it. Chest to chest, with her fingers grazing its damaged shell.

The pahaalusk's eyes shone. They were round with fear. They looked directly at her. Something gleamed inside them, like little pinpricks, and she realized it was her reflection. But it was more than that, too. Images. Memories. Lalani's mother kissing her forehead. The long-haired girl—Veyda, yes, that was her name—taking her hand. Cade, drenched with rain and looking at Drum. Ships sailing north.

Kill it. You share nothing with this creature.

"We share this boat," she said.

She loosened her grip.

She sat back. Water soaked her dress.

She breathed deeply.

She remembered who she was now.

Her name was Lalani Sarita.

She looked at the pahaalusk. It laid its head on her lap. "If we die, we die together," she whispered.

* * *

Lalani navigated with the cracked paddle, despite the throbbing in her hand and the stubbornness of the boat.

She had hunger pangs, but no food. She didn't know how to hunt. She hadn't packed a single thing. She didn't know where she was going.

She'd left her dying mother behind to set sail on a foolish mission.

She was a stupid twelve-year-old girl with a splinter in her hand.

All these feelings and others—the speared wallecta, the feel of Drum's hand on her arm, the empty sockets in Ellseth's face—gathered inside her. She tried not to cry. She was a girl on a mission, like Ziva. But she was a sailor, not a stowaway. She was doing what her father and others had done before her. Had any of *them* cried? She doubted it. She wanted to be brave like Ziva. But her chest ached with sorrow and soon, a tear. Then another and another. She sniffled. The pahaalusk blinked up at her.

"I'm a stupid girl," she said.

She and Veyda used to cry over their lost fathers. They would sob on each other's shoulders. There was no shame in crying—was there? Lalani let the tears fall but didn't stop paddling.

A person can't cry forever. When the well finally ran dry, Lalani's face felt puffy and sore. She moved the paddle through the water with no idea if she was getting anywhere.

Thirst replaced hunger. She scooped a handful of water from the sea and tried to drink it, but it burned her tongue and she spit it out. Waves of nausea washed over her for a while after that.

The pahaalusk didn't seem as moved by dreams of food and water. It slept peacefully in its shell.

Lalani's arms were thin, wiry, and strong, but soon they were so sore that every dip of the paddle, no matter how small, felt like a challenge. She kept going for as long as she could, but it seemed that she was making no headway. She put the paddle down and rubbed her arms.

She thought of her mother and Veyda. And she thought of food, food, food.

She yawned. When she turned her mind away from home and hunger and focused on the boat and water, she found something peaceful about it. The way the water rocked her back and forth. The quiet lapping. No thudding of Drum's boots. No wails from poor little Toppi. No pounding of rain.

She lay down next to the pahaalusk. More water had collected in the boat, but she didn't care. She wanted rest, even if it soaked her dress and hair. It was a tight fit, but she was small enough to situate her body in a comfortable position. Well, as comfortable as one can be in a scouting boat. She imagined her mother next to her. One, two, one, two.

She fell asleep quickly. She dreamed she was a cloud—white, puffy, and light—floating over a green island. The grass was so tall and lush that it tickled her. Yellow flowers bloomed everywhere, and she was weightless. No responsibilities, no thoughts except how high she could soar. Higher, higher. Sunlight warmed her and all was well.

Lalani couldn't say why she opened her eyes. There was no jarring against the boat, no loud *thwack*. She opened her eyes anyway. She wasn't prepared for what she saw.

A woman. Well, the head of a woman. Enormous. Larger than the boat, even. Her eyes glistened like crystals; that was the first thing Lalani noticed. Then a long, straight nose, which pointed to two perfectly shaped blue lips. Her skin was pale, virtually translucent. Lalani had never seen skin like that. Then again, she'd never seen a woman rise from water.

The woman's hair: long, wet, nearly white. In Sanlagita the rain had plastered hair to faces in messy nests, but this creature's hair looked smooth and silky. It ran down either side of her face in waves. She had no arms, not that Lalani could see anyway. But her neck—was that a neck? No. It was a body—a body like a fish, but long and curled, stretching forever just under the surface of the water. Lalani couldn't see where it ended.

"Am I dreaming?" said Lalani.

"Is it possible to dream with your eyes open?" the creature asked. Her voice was light and lilting, like bubbles rising from a stream.

"I don't know," Lalani said. She placed her hand on the pahaalusk shell to remind her of reality.

But what if this was reality, too?

"Who are you?" the sea-woman asked.

"Lalani Sarita."

"*What* are you?"

"A girl." Lalani paused. "Who are you?" she added, as politely as possible.

The woman's eyebrows, nearly invisible, furrowed, as if this was a foolish question.

"I'm Ditasa-Ulod," she replied. She swept her eyes over the scouting boat. "What are you doing in my sea?"

"I'm . . . looking for something. Someone? I don't know, really. I just . . ." Lalani had no real answer. *I'm a stupid girl. I don't know what I'm doing. I ruined my village and I left. I don't know what I was thinking. I didn't even pack food.* But she was too frightened to say exactly what was on her mind.

The creature swished this way and that. A small wake rippled across the water's surface. "Who are you looking for?" she asked.

Lalani swallowed. Oh, her throat was so parched. "Fei Diwata?" she said finally.

"Fei Diwata? Ha!" *Swish, swish.* "Fei Diwata has no interest in a human girl. Fei Diwata has not been the same since a mindoren stole her udyo. She no longer trusts anyone. Especially not an *outsider.*"

Lalani's mind traveled back to the moment Ellseth cured her wounded knee with his staff. She remembered the strange images that had flooded over her: A single tree. Piercing screams. *My udyo! My udyo!* A man with wide, light eyes, who she now recognized as Ellseth.

"Fei Diwata sees into the hearts of all living things," Ditasa-Ulod continued. "And she prizes one virtue above all else. If she looks into your heart and doesn't see it there, you will die. Do you want to die?"

Lalani couldn't speak.

"But it's no matter anyway," Ditasa-Ulod continued. *Swish, swish*. "You'd have to cross my sea first. I've seen humans here before, but they were much bigger than you, and their boats were much more seaworthy." She lowered her body into the water and swam around the scouting boat, as elegant as a ribbon of smoke. Her hair floated around her. "Your vessel is small, so it will be easy to drown you."

She draped her stately tail over the bow of the boat. It rocked under the weight.

"To . . . drown me?" Lalani said. The words barely escaped.

"Of course," Ditasa-Ulod replied. Her tail glistened, sleek and black. She rocked the boat again and the pahaalusk opened its eyes, confused.

Lalani clutched the sides of the boat, even though it was clear that this eel-woman could tip it over with no effort at all.

And that's exactly what she did.

One moment Lalani was breathing air and the next, her mouth and nose filled with water and she didn't know which way was up. Her eyes were open and burning. Her arms flailed frantically, searching for something to grab onto. Her fingertips brushed the boat and then the scaled body of Ditasa-Ulod, and she was thrust down through the water—*whoosh*. She kicked, but it did no good. She turned and twisted, going nowhere. Something hit her face and she jerked back, only to discover that it was the pouch still around her neck, and then she saw something coming toward her through the clear water and she thought this is it, this is how it ends, but it wasn't Ditasa-Ulod—no, it was something else, something round and familiar—it was the pahaalusk, moving its webbed feet effortlessly and diving in her direction. She wrapped her arms around its shell and held on tightly. When they broke the surface of the sea together, she tried to take a big, deep breath but erupted into a painful coughing fit instead. Water choked her lungs and throat. It spilled from her. Her eyes and nose were on fire. She coughed and coughed and coughed. Finally she gathered herself, and clutching the pahaalusk with one hand, she wiped the hair away from her face with the other and looked around. She and the pahaalusk were floating together in a wide expanse of sea.

It was quiet.

Very, very quiet.

Lalani turned in every direction, panicked.

Where was the eel-woman?

"Hello!" Lalani yelled, her throat burning.

Perhaps that was foolish, but there was no hiding here. And if Ditasa-Ulod were going to attack again, Lalani wanted to know sooner rather than later. Why drag it out?

"Ditasa-Ulod!" called Lalani, just as a small wave appeared.

Lalani waited.

When Ditasa-Ulod's head rose right in front of her, she wasn't as frightened as she'd been before.

"You're still alive," the eel-woman said calmly. "The pahaalusk rescued you."

"We've rescued each other," Lalani replied. She glanced down at her arms, draped across the pahaalusk's back, and discovered that her skin was clean. The mud had completely washed away.

"It will be even easier to destroy you than your little boat," Ditasa-Ulod said. She may have shrugged, if she'd had shoulders.

"Can I ask you a question?" Lalani said.

"A question?"

"Yes. If you're going to drown me anyway, surely you can answer a question." Lalani blinked and clutched the pahaalusk's shell. "You rule this sea, right?"

"Of course."

"So you know everything that happens here?"

"Everything."

"I want to know—that is, I'd *like* to know . . ." A messy web of emotions swam through her. "Did you know my father? He was a sailor and he probably died here like the others."

"If your father sailed my sea, then I know him."

Lalani told Ditasa-Ulod her father's name and described what he looked like. She told all she knew about his ship, and the other men with him, including Veyda's father.

"Oh, yes," the eel-woman finally said. "I remember him."

"You do?"

"Certainly. I remember every creature." *Swish, swish.* "He drifted for days in his huge vessel. The other men were confused by the mist and went overboard. And this man, this 'father' you speak of, soon ran out of food and water. After he died, his ship floated aimlessly. All the creatures came out to admire it. Eventually, though, it was destroyed."

"He died all by himself," Lalani said. A statement, not a question.

"Yes," Ditasa-Ulod replied. She lifted the tip of her magnificent tail and crashed it against the water. The waves were instant and enormous. Lalani, holding tight, sailed into the air with the pahaalusk.

She curled her body around the animal as best she could. The curve of her back hit the surface of the sea—*crash!*—and she spun, spun, spun underneath, losing her grip and unfurling like a fisherman's net until her arms finally found themselves and pushed frantically through the water. Her shoulder rammed into something.

A rockbed.

She stared at it with round, bloodshot eyes, and let the waves push her up.

She raised her head. No coughing this time.

She blinked and blinked, not sure of what she was seeing.

The shore. Trees. Green. Land.

She imagined Ditasa-Ulod's tail rising behind her, ready to drown her, but instead of turning around, Lalani pulled herself forward and didn't look back, even as the scouting boat emerged behind her.

YOU ARE A GOYUK

Imagine you are very small. Smaller than a fingernail. You have four wings, eight legs, and a long, piercing snout, which is a brilliant shade of yellow.

Here is how you fly: you tuck all your legs underneath your belly to conserve energy, then you move your wings rapidly in succession. You buzz, but it is very faint and can't be helped.

If you were any other insect, you would use your snout to feed—sweet nectar from the flowers, or blood from the animals—but you are not like any other insect. You are not an insect at all. You are a sorceress.

Don't laugh. It's true. Centuries ago, your ancestors—the goyuk—faced a decision: What would you become? They could have chosen to be giants. Beasts as big as mountains. But no—the goyuk are much too clever. The goyuk understand something that other creatures do not: The mightiest are often the smallest. So the goyuk made themselves as small as they could, and when they wished to conquer their part of the island, they landed on their enemies' beefy necks and bit them. An illness traveled from your snout and into their skin and they fell, one by one, until there were none left.

It takes five days to kill a giant.

Your victims see and hear things that aren't there. Their heads throb with pain. Weaker and weaker they become until, finally, they can no longer walk and they fall into a deep, deep sleep, forever. Your power is a thing of beauty.

The goyuk hives are magnificent now, and everyone has a purpose. Today your purpose is to search for intruders and kill them. You are sent off on this task every third day, and there is never an intruder, but you are a good and loyal worker, so you are always ready.

The older goyuk say there is no delight in killing. It's just something that must be done to protect your part of the island. Intruders grow like weeds unless they are stopped. The goyuk should know, being intruders themselves. But you have a secret. You have never stopped an intruder, and you want to use your bright yellow snout at least once.

You buzz and you think: What if, one day, the goyuk swarm covers the entire island? Wouldn't that be lovely?

This is what you are thinking when you see something strange. At first you don't believe it, but yes—it's true. There is an intruder on the shore. You can ready your dagger at last.

You study her.

You buzz closer.

Her eyes say: I am lost.

Her eyes say: I am scared.

Your eyes (of which there are thirty) say: I'm coming for you.

A Distant Shore

The insect bite woke Lalani up. Then a light nudge on the shoulder. She hadn't realized she'd fallen asleep until she lifted her heavy eyelids and blinked at the sky. She swatted the bug away. It pulled its bright yellow stinger out of her skin and disappeared into the slanting sunlight, which was half blocked by a girl hovering over her—the one who'd nudged her shoulder, presumably.

"Where are your horns?" the girl said.

Lalani ached from head to toe. The splinter. Her arms. Her legs. And now, this bug bite on her elbow. She groaned and said, "What?"

The girl's face was shadowed so Lalani couldn't make out her features. She peered down at Lalani from behind a curtain of hair.

"Your horns," the girl said. "You don't have any."

Lalani lifted herself up. "Why would I have horns?"

But she saw the answer as soon as she asked the question. Two horns—thick and sturdy—jutted from the girl's head. Just like Ellseth's.

"What kind of creature are you?" the girl asked. She looked toward the sea, as if it held an answer.

"I'm a human," Lalani said.

"I've never seen a human like you before."

"I'm a girl."

The horned creature raised an eyebrow suspiciously. "What are you called?"

"My name is Lalani Sarita. What are you called?"

"Usoa."

They stared at each other.

"How old are you?" Lalani asked.

"How should I know?" Usoa replied.

Lalani rubbed her arm. The insect bite was swollen already. And she was hungry.

"What's wrong?" Usoa asked. "Are you sick?"

"No. I'm hungry."

"Is that why you gathered all that food?"

"What food?"

Usoa motioned to a small pyramid of bright orange fruit atop a nest of leaves. It was clear the fruit had been picked and placed carefully.

"That's not mine," Lalani said, even as her mouth watered.

"Well, it's not mine, either."

Lalani squeezed her eyes shut then opened them and focused. The horizon in front of her was endless and shimmering. Bright plants, green leaves, brown tree trunks, blue sky, white clouds. If Veyda were here, she could make all the salve she wanted. And what if she found the yellow flower? What if?

"Where is the pahaalusk?" Lalani asked.

Usoa tilted her head, confused and silent.

"Never mind," Lalani replied, scanning the shore.

There was no sign of the animal. It had saved her and now it was gone.

Please be alive, Lalani thought.

"It must be yours," Usoa continued. "The food, I mean."

Lalani wanted to weep over the pahaalusk—over everything, really—and immediately scour the island for Fei Diwata and the yellow flowers, but she was starving. She snatched fruit from the pyramid and barely took time to peel the skin. As she chewed those first few bites, she forgot about the pain in her body, the sting as the juice nestled into her splinter. She ate and ate and ate until she felt nauseous, and Usoa stood over her, hand on her hip.

"Is that how all human girls eat osabana?" Usoa asked, scrunching her nose.

Osabana. Lalani didn't want to forget a single detail, just in case she survived to tell her story to Veyda and Hetsbi.

"I've never had it before," Lalani said. She stood and wiped her face with her hands. "It's delicious. You should try it."

"I prefer tree bark, or sprigs of grass." Usoa paused. "What are you doing here? Are you looking for the mountain?"

Lalani hesitated, not sure how much she should say. "I was told there was a mountain guarded by a creature called Fei Diwata," Lalani finally said. The splinter was on fire. She sucked on her hand, but it did nothing to dull the pain. "And she has yellow flowers."

"If you're trying to get there, you won't make it. You'll probably die," Usoa said. "Everyone else has."

Lalani dropped her hand. "Everyone?"

"Yes," Usoa said. "Let me see that."

The flesh around the splinter was red and swollen, the splice of wood deeply embedded. Lalani placed her hand in Usoa's open palm; Usoa poked at it with her finger.

"I used to get splinters when I was a young mindoren," said Usoa. "Mostly in my knees, from climbing trees. But I'd always get the best twigs and bark." Usoa poked and poked at the splinter again and turned Lalani's hand over in hers. "I picked them as gifts for my mother." She looked up. "I'm going to take it out. Brace yourself. Focus on something else if you can. And don't look."

Lalani turned away and focused on the spattering of osabana peels.

"My mother was very good with splinters," Usoa said.

Lalani's eyes pooled as the pain seared through her arm. "Does your mother still live here?"

Usoa didn't respond right away. She nodded toward distant hills. "I roam with a small herd over there, but we mostly keep to ourselves. That's how the mindoren are."

Lalani thought of Ellseth then. How the mindoren had tied him to a tree and taken his eyes. What if this was a trick and Usoa planned to capture her? What if *she* was tied to a tree? What if *she* lost her eyes?

The searing pain of the splinter breaking through her skin was almost unbearable. But Lalani didn't make a sound. She held her closed fist to her chest and breathed deeply.

"Something else got you, too," Usoa said. "You have a bite on your arm."

"Yes." Lalani studied the soft part of her hand where the splinter had been. "A bug with a yellow stinger."

Usoa's face darkened. "Yellow stinger?"

"Yes."

"That must have been a goyuk," said Usoa quietly. "They have hives many miles from here."

"It stung a little, but it doesn't hurt much," Lalani said. She studied the creases in Usoa's forehead—a tell. "What's wrong?"

"Oh. Nothing. I just didn't know the goyuk traveled this far."

"They must be more powerful than they look," Lalani said.

"Yes," Usoa agreed. "Yes. They are."

In Sanlagita

It could have been worse, the villagers said. Kahna showed mercy. Yes, the Pasas and the menyoro were dead. Villagers were bruised and battered. Lalani Sarita was missing. Houses were splintered, crops were buried, but Kahna largely spared them.

Still.

There were not enough shek to provide thread. Many of them had perished.

Most of the crops were gone.

Even if the weather straightened itself out, it would take years to recover from the devastation, and who had years?

Certainly not Lalani's mother, whose fever rose under Lo Yuzi's roof. Lalani was right: she had grown sicker, too sick to be any good to Drum or Kul. They had been happy to make her someone else's problem.

As for everyone else? They said their benedictions.

They asked Kahna for mercy.

Veyda cared for Lalani's mother, as promised.

Cade secretly visited the northern shore.

And one man considered the now-vacant seat of the menyoro. He turned thoughts over and over. He watched the villagers. Saw the fear in their eyes, poor creatures. They were lost without a leader.

He would give them one.

YOU ARE WHENBO

Imagine you are a whenbo root. You are spindly and misshapen and you only grow from one certain patch of land. You don't drink water or sunlight. Only souls.

So many of them come to you. They wash up on the shore. Their bodies are dead, but their spirits wander. They search for a place to nestle. They are drawn to you. You beckon them. *Here. Here. Rest.*

Once they've burrowed themselves into the earth, they become one with you. And together, you sprout. You find joy in stretching yourself out of soil and toward the sky, but there is little happiness in it for the souls. Only sorrow for a lost cause. A failed journey. They tell you: *We wanted to go north. We thought we could make it. But we did not survive.*

And you say: *Rest now and be quiet. Fold yourself into the bristle of my trunk. Whisper your name into it. The whenbo will not forget you. Perhaps you were not able to cross—perhaps you did not have what Isa wanted—but stay here, with me. Do not seek vengeance. Quiet yourself. Forget the journey.*

Only Mother Isa knows who is destined to cross.

It was not your destiny to survive.

Your destiny is here, with the whenbo.

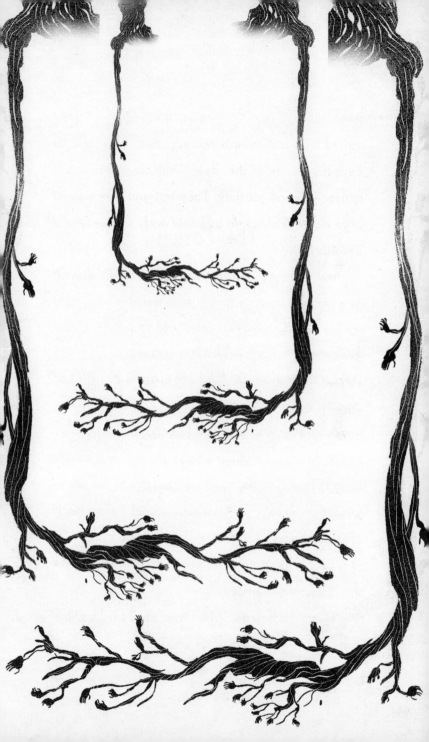

The Forest

Lalani didn't know why Usoa decided to help her. Perhaps she was bored or lonely, or maybe she simply had nothing better to do. Whatever the reason, the young mindoren offered to walk with Lalani, and Lalani readily accepted. Why would she refuse? She was much more likely to reach Fei Diwata with a mindoren by her side—someone who knew the island and could protect her if needed. Assuming Usoa was willing to protect her.

"I will walk with you for five days," Usoa said. "After that, I'll return to my herd."

"Okay," Lalani agreed. They'd already started walking

north, side by side, toward the edge of a forest. "Will we reach Fei Diwata in five days?"

Usoa glanced at Lalani, then away. "Maybe. I don't know. I've never been to her mountain. People have tried to journey there, but . . ."

"But what?"

Usoa didn't respond.

Soon they settled into a steady pace. Everything on Isa appeared beautifully serene. *Maybe I'll make it to the mountain after all*, Lalani thought. She wondered how so many men had died here when it seemed so peaceful. The forest, when they reached it, wasn't frightening like the one on Sanlagita. It teemed with small animals—busy four-legged creatures with bushy tails, who leaped from tree to tree and scrambled so quickly Lalani barely had time to study them; birds, too, different than the ones on Sanlagita, but just as silent; and whiskered little things with prickly backs who dashed across the forest floor playfully.

Usoa named each animal for her.

"Balawuk," she said, pointing at the bushy tail.

"Ebee," she said of the playful prickly creatures.

"Gigo and quitzi." She gestured to the birds in the trees.

Nothing here seemed dangerous. Certainly not deadly.

Perhaps the island was once fierce but had become docile.

Perhaps the island had suffered somehow, but that had passed and all was well now.

Perhaps the creatures had decided to open their arms to visitors.

Either way, there was no turning back.

What was it her mother liked to say?

The only way out is through.

Thinking of her mother conjured up terrifying possibilities.

What if she had already died and Lalani hadn't been there?

"Don't step on these mounds," Usoa said when they

reached a cluster of strange little hills in their path. There were many of them, Lalani noticed, scattered haphazardly across the forest floor. "There will be more as we go farther north. You have to walk around them."

"Why?" Lalani asked.

"They're nunso mounds."

"What are nunso mounds?"

"You have much to learn about this place," Usoa replied.

The air was clearer here, with only an occasional breeze. Not too warm. Not too cold. Lalani picked up a small branch. She swung it in front of her but soon grew bored and tossed it away. The trees were far apart, so their trail was wide. The next time she saw an ebee, she crouched and called to it.

"They're very friendly," Usoa said, standing next to her. She made a clucking noise with her tongue. The ebee looked toward them, whiskers twitching. It was bigger than a wallecta, but not overly large. Small enough to carry.

"Can I pick it up?" Lalani asked.

Usoa shrugged. "If it'll let you."

"Do they bite?"

"Not usually," Usoa replied. "But they have teeth, and anything with teeth can bite. That's what my mother always said."

Lalani mimicked the sound Usoa had made. The ebee walked toward her tentatively with its spikes resting flat on its back.

"The spikes are for defense," Usoa said. "When ebee feel safe, they're just as furry as a balawuk. My mother used to say ebee were the smartest creatures on the island, because they sense danger better than anything. That's when their spikes come out."

The ebee was within reach now. Lalani picked it up in one careful, quiet movement, then stood with it cradled in her arms. Its ears were small, round, and thin as leaves. Its short snout was topped with a pink, triangular nose. Usoa tickled its soft belly. Lalani ran a finger behind its ear. The ebee's eyes closed.

"My mother has a saying, too," Lalani said. "She says, 'The only way out is through.'"

"I like that."

"Do you still live with your mother? You never really answered before."

Usoa paused. "My mother is dead."

"Oh." Lalani frowned. "I'm sorry. Was she sick?"

"No. She was killed, trying to make amends."

Usoa's Story

What is your first memory? Mine is the image of a talon.

I was born on a grassy highland and spent the first three years of my life there, in a bed of leaves my mother collected for me. The talon shared my nest. It was sharp. The same length as I was, with a curved hook at the end. My mother swatted my hand away if I reached for it. Afterward, she would kiss my fingers and explain.

"That doesn't belong to us, my love," she'd say. "We must take care of it until we can bring it back to its owner."

I never asked who the owner was. Not at first. I was just

a child, and I didn't care about such things. I just wanted to hold it. The talon was made of shining ebony, and I was enchanted by the way it reflected the moonlight. I wished my horns were made of ebony, too. Soon, however, my mind focused on other things, like helping my mother with the newborn mindoren and gathering the softest leaves for their nests, and I forgot about it.

One night, my mother wrapped the talon in a satchel made of balawuk hide. Two female mindoren—Oona and Simona—stood beside her. Their eyes were dark. Their brows, furrowed.

"What's going on?" I asked. I was young, but never afraid to ask my mother questions. We were a pair, the two of us. A mother mindoren with a heart as big as the sea, and her curious daughter, full of wonder and questions.

"It's time for us to return this to its owner," my mother said.

Her voice was quiet and wary. I'd never heard it sound that way.

Once the talon was tightly wrapped, she slipped the

satchel on her shoulder and kneeled in front of me.

"This talon belongs to a bai," she said. "It was cut from her foot many years ago by a wicked mindoren thief. He stole many things while he lived among us. After he was banished from our herd, we vowed to return all his treasures. This is the last item remaining—that we know of, at least. Once this is returned, we will have made our peace."

You would have thought I'd be afraid, but I wasn't. My heart leaped with joy. My mother and I, on a quest to return a stolen treasure!

"I thought all the bai were dead," I said, hardly able to contain my excitement. "How will we return it?"

"It's true, the bai are no longer with us. But we still have no right to keep it. We will bury it under a pachenka tree as a gesture of our regret."

"When do we leave?" I asked.

My mother stood. She smiled down at me.

"I'm sorry, my love, but this is not a journey for a young mindoren," she said. "You will have to wait for me. I won't be long. I'll bring you pachenka leaves as a keepsake. And a bai feather, if I can find one."

But the idea of leaves and feathers was of little consolation to me when I had my heart set on a grand adventure.

I told my mother I would wait.

It was the first time I lied to her.

And the last.

I followed them. I darted behind trees. I slept in hollows. I made myself invisible. It was two adventures in one—not only was I returning a mighty talon to its rightful owner, I was also an infiltrator, and a skilled one at that.

My mother never knew I was there.

It took several days to reach the pachenka grove. I'd heard stories of the bai and their enormous pachenka nests, but I'd never visited the grove before. They were the tallest and widest trees I had ever seen, and even though I'd spent my whole life admiring the talon, I never appreciated how vast the bai must have been until I saw where they once lived.

I crouched out of sight, as close as I could get without being discovered, and watched my mother and her friends kneel and bury the talon. Even from where I hid, I could see the looks of reverence and respect on their faces. They weren't the ones who had stolen it, but they felt responsible nonetheless. That's how the mindoren are—we have a strong sense of loyalty and community. What happens to one happens to all.

That's what I thought at the time, anyway.

None of us expected what came next.

It happened so fast.

A gust of wind knocked me over. That was the first thing. When I sat up, I realized that it wasn't just wind. It was a bird. A *bai*. You can imagine how confused I was. I believed all the bai were dead. But I knew right away that's what it was. A bai, charging down from nowhere. It had all its talons. I know, because I saw all twelve of them. Six on each claw. Sharp, pointed, curved like hooks. I counted them. I don't know how, but I did. I wanted to know—was this the bai who'd been attacked by the mindoren thief? One, two, three, four, five, six. I counted all the way to twelve as the talons sliced into my mother.

"You stole my sister's talon!" the bai squawked, so loudly that I covered both ears. I was still crouched, frozen from fear. I couldn't look away from my mother. But her companions? Oh, they had no trouble turning a blind eye. They ran. Both of them. They ran as the bai killed my mother. This creature, this beast, long believed dead, squawked her own name as my mother died. *I am Bai-Vinca!*, she said. As if my mother needed to know. As if my *mother* was the evil one.

I found my footing. I leaped from my hiding place, screaming my mother's name.

"She is Morena!" I cried. "She is Morena!"

I screamed her name to no one, for Bai-Vinca had disappeared just as suddenly as she'd come.

I fell to my mother's side. I was just a girl. I had never seen blood before, and you can't imagine how much I saw that day.

"Mama," I said. "Mama."

But it was too late.

She was gone.

My mother never knew I was there.

I did not return home. Why would I? My herd was full of cowards. They left my mother to die. They didn't even try to save her. I made a vow that I would do what they had not. I would grow up strong and fierce. I would dedicate my life to a single purpose: avenging my mother's death. I've spent years preparing myself.

You probably think I cried that day. You probably think I've cried since. But you are wrong. I haven't shed a single tear. Vengeance powers me, not sorrow. I will mourn when justice is served.

No one should die alone, Lalani.

Not even Bai-Vinca.

And she won't.

I will be there.

Beintai

The farther Lalani and Usoa walked, the heavier the ebee seemed. The creature pawed at the pouch around Lalani's neck, and its spikes pushed against the tender part of her thumb. But she didn't want to let the animal go. It was such a sweet little thing, nestled in the crook of her arms, and after Usoa's story, she wanted something gentle to look at. Lalani was thinking of her own mother, of course. But mostly she thought of her father, who had also died alone.

She wanted to tell Usoa *My father died alone,* but she couldn't get the words out. She was afraid she'd cry, and she wanted to be brave like Usoa or Ziva, especially now that the trees were getting denser.

"Where does Bai-Vinca live?" Lalani asked as she stepped around one of the mounds.

"In the pachenka grove just beyond the whenbo forest," Usoa answered. She kept her eyes straight ahead. Lalani noticed the bulging muscles in Usoa's legs. She looked strong, hearty, like she could cleave a rock if she wanted to.

Lalani adjusted the ebee in her arms. "What's the whenbo forest?"

Usoa paused. "You'll find out."

They continued on in silence. The trees were bent at odd angles here. And some of them were leafless in a sea of green.

The ebee opened its eyes. The spikes on its forehead immediately jutted forward and Lalani flinched, startled. The ebee looked toward the path ahead and hissed so loudly that Lalani dropped it. By the time it hit the ground, all its spikes were out. It scurried madly in the opposite direction.

Lalani raised her eyebrows at Usoa. "That was strange."

Usoa looked around, eyes narrowed, then continued walking.

"Is Bai-Vinca worse than Ditasa-Ulod?" Lalani asked.

"In what way?" Usoa asked.

"Ditasa-Ulod tried to drown me."

"She tries to kill all humans. I'm surprised you're still alive."

Here was another strange tree. Thin, wiry, with oddly colored bark. And more mounds for them to sidestep.

Usoa continued, "Ditasa-Ulod says humans will destroy us, if we allow them on our land. She doesn't like outsiders. She's just one of many."

"One of many what?"

"Creatures here who despise you."

Lalani's skin prickled. It was so, so quiet.

The trees were even closer together here. They became increasingly gnarled. Lalani wasn't sure if Usoa was one of the things she was supposed to be afraid of. How was she to know whom to trust? She'd trusted Ellseth, and look what had happened. She kept her eyes forward and tried to swallow the thumping of her heart, all the while thinking: What if Usoa is leading me into the forest so she can kill me? What if she ties me up and gouges out my eyes?

Twisted trunks surrounded them. The sky—slate gray and unchanging—hovered above them. Leafless branches dipped and bent in every direction. When Lalani was little, one of the Oragleo sisters had broken her arm and that's what the branches reminded her of. Veyda had made a sling that reached around the girl's neck so the broken arm could nestle there safely. But there was no cradle for these trees. And nothing felt safe about them.

"These trees—" Lalani had the crazy feeling that they were watching her. Listening. She stared at the ground, even though Veyda always said it was best to keep your chin up so you didn't run into something you didn't expect.

"They are called whenbo," said Usoa. "Each of them has a name."

"A name?"

"Yes. Each one."

The forest seemed to take a deep breath.

"Watch," Usoa said. "I'll show you."

Usoa approached one of the whenbo. She put her ear to its trunk and closed her eyes.

"This one is called Unlo," she said. She pressed her ear against another. "This one is Hareton." At the next tree, Usoa said: "Esdel."

Lalani's heart loosened and unspooled.

Surely not Cade's brother Esdel. How would Usoa know his name?

Lalani thought of Cade, gazing out at the water on Sailing Day as his brother disappeared into the mist.

It was a coincidence. Usoa could have come up with that name off the top of her head. It didn't mean anything.

But then Usoa put her ear to another trunk, her horn resting on the bark.

"Beintai," she said.

Beintai.

Lalani's father.

The Whenbo Forest

The moment Lalani heard her father's name, the whenbo forest became something different. She was no longer frightened. She ran to the tree with her father's name so suddenly that Usoa stumbled back, confused. Lalani wrapped her arms around the trunk and listened. Usoa was telling the truth. She heard it. Faintly. Lifting from the ridges in the trunk like wisps of smoke.

Beintai.

Beintai.

Lalani didn't care that she was crying. If Usoa thought she was weak or cowardly, so be it. This tree had her father's name. There it was, again and again, in her ear.

A thousand memories rushed back. The way her father smelled of the sea after days on the water. His expression when he looked at her mother, and hers when she looked at him. A life before Drum and Kul, when she and Veyda played together and knew nothing else but the comfort of their homes and the love of their parents. An endless spool of questions wove through her mind: What would her father think of her being here? Would he be proud, or would he think she was useless and stupid? What would her life be like if he had lived? Why had *she* survived the Veiled Sea when he had not?

Usoa placed a hand on Lalani's shoulder, so lightly that neither of them truly felt it.

"The whenbo," Usoa paused, as if hesitant to go on. "They carry the souls of the dead."

The whenbo carry the souls of the dead.

Lalani clutched the tree tighter. The pouch with Ellseth's arrowhead in it caught on a sliver of bark, as if connecting them.

"My father is Beintai," said Lalani. "Does this mean he's trapped inside?"

"Not trapped," Usoa explained. "It's his soul. It washed up on the shore and now the tree cares for his spirit."

Lalani wanted to cry out *I don't understand, I don't understand*, because it made no sense. But nothing made sense. The bloody cloth from her mother's pricked finger. Toppi, sick in his mother's arms. Veyda and her empty basket. Kahna cracking open.

Lalani pushed herself away from the whenbo named Beintai and ran to another tree.

She wanted to hear their names. *All* their names.

Boracleo.

Boracleo. Lalani searched her memory, but nothing surfaced. Then again, this tree felt old and weary under the soft skin of her aching hand. Who knew how long it had stood there?

She moved to another.

Ulan.

And another.

Giam.

And another.

Xan.

Nykal.

Miriso.

Edene.

Usoa called to her, told her to slow down, to stop, but Lalani couldn't. She wanted—no, needed—to hear them all.

Mosan, Verale, Ruwan, Isseri, Dynel, Oldis, Imlor.

She wanted to hear the name of Veyda's father.

Aemu, Danolo, Imthi, Wartas.

Torip, Makhelo, Mysay, Otasy.

She darted like a bird from one tree to the next until she heard another name she knew. Not Veyda's father, but *Isagani.*

Yes, she remembered him well.

Isagani was one of the Pasa cousins. He was tall and lean, with skin like sparkling bronze. Handsome. Strong.

He was a skilled carpenter, so he had helped build ships and houses. She and Veyda had spied on him one afternoon, a few years ago, as he lifted felled logs and put them into place. Someone was getting a new house that day—who was it? Lalani didn't remember. But the memory of Isagani was round and clear.

"When I grow up, I'm going to have a husband like Isagani," Veyda had whispered. The two of them were in the wildflower patch, which gave them a clear view, but hid them behind tall plants and blossoms. Veyda always seemed to be drawn to these particular weeds, but Lalani found them maddening, the way they scratched her legs and arms and made her eyes water.

"I'm not going to have a husband," Lalani had said. "I'm going to run away like Ziva, and live on Isa."

Veyda never bothered to remind her of Ziva's fate.

And now here Lalani was, listening to one of the whenbo whisper Isagani's name. She and Veyda had been hopeful the day he set sail, even though their fathers' deaths should have taught them better. If anyone would survive, it would be Isagani. He was strong and determined. He treated the women with respect. He'd often catch girls like Lalani and Veyda watching him; when he did, he winked or stuck out his tongue. Sometimes he picked a piece of fruit and tossed it for them to catch. Surely someone like Isagani would return, they'd thought.

Then one week passed. A month. Two months. Eventually, he faded into memory like the others.

Lalani pressed her forehead against the tree.

"I'm sorry, Isagani," she whispered.

She was so lost in the past that she forgot herself.

When she lifted her head, Usoa was no longer visible.

Lalani's heart leaped into her throat.

"Usoa!" she called. "Usoa!"

She stepped away from Isagani as if the tree had suddenly become something hot and dangerous to the touch. Her eyes widened as she saw the whenbo forest for the first time for what it really was—a gathering of tortured souls.

"Usoa! Usoa!" she cried. Her face was wet with tears. "Usoa! Usoa!"

You're such a stupid girl, she thought. Look what you've done now—you've gotten lost. Again.

Lalani turned this way and that trying to figure out where she'd come from, but now everything looked the same and she wasn't even sure which tree was Isagani anymore. She leaned into the whenbo next to her. If she found Isagani and worked her way back to Boracleo, she could get her bearings again.

Marico.

She moved to another.

Avelin.

She stumbled on. The next tree whispered *Sai*. Then *Ciato*. Then *Iarn* and *Prasad*. She'd never heard these names before, which meant she'd not been this way. She shot like a wallecta across the whenbo grove, panicked, even though she knew Sai and Iarn—they'd sailed when she was very young; Sai had a light streak against his dark hair, and she remembered it blowing in the breeze before the ocean swallowed him—but that didn't matter at this moment, because she was lost in a forest of ghosts, scrambling to find one of the names she'd heard before, hurrying to discover Boracleo again, because he was the closest to the trail, wasn't he? But there were only new names, more and more souls.

"Usoa!" she cried. "Usoa!"

She found a small, unfamiliar clearing and stood very still, listening. She itched the bite on her elbow. Her head throbbed.

There.

A sound.

She held her breath.

The sound soared through the silence of the whenbo forest.

Something was wailing. A baby? Lalani thought of Toppi. Was he here? No, that didn't make sense.

It was something else.

An animal?

Lalani walked in a slow circle, then stopped to listen

again. Where was the sound coming from? From all around, it seemed. But that couldn't be. The creature was somewhere. She pictured the animal, whatever it was: small, cradled in leaves and thickets, fat tears dampening the fur around its eyes. Waiting for someone to pick it up and say *shhh-shhh-everything will be fine*, and here she was, a girl with perfectly good arms for lifting and a perfectly tuned voice for comforting, and how could she possibly keep walking and turn her back?

Lalani shuddered. Inexplicably, her mind drifted to the day she'd fallen on the rocks, when Maddux had said she was a kind girl.

The animal's cries, once again, filled the air.

This time Lalani moved quickly.

YOU ARE THE YOOTAH

Imagine all the ugly things inside your soul collecting in the center of your heart. Imagine them as a churning cloud. The cloud is red—deep red, the color of blood—and weightless, because there is no love or kindness to give it substance. It eats everything you find beautiful and spits it out until the pieces are so small and shredded that they no longer exist. Rage, resentment, jealousy, and hatred are all that is left behind.

You are the yootah.

You feed on hands.

Not just *any* hands.

They must be warm.

They must be lavender.

They must get close enough to your hungry teeth.

But no one would ever come to you with open arms and open palms. Not the way you look. They must be tricked first. As a yootah, you know that the best way to trick someone is to take the shape of something else. Something harmless.

You also know that trust has a color: lavender. Not everyone can see it. Lavender hands have all kinds of things trapped inside. Good things, like mothers, and bad things, like heartache. Trust shines brilliantly. The light is brightest in the hands, because that's the first thing people offer. That's why they taste the sweetest.

How do you spot that lavender light? You listen for its song and then you change your own tune. You find something good, and you mimic it. You are a sentient cloud, and a shape-shifter. You can change your appearance and your song. Today you sound like an injured animal. You slipped your swirling form into a blanket and placed yourself under a tree. A breeze of lavender moves toward you. It shines faintly, which means that this creature does not trust easily. No matter. The light is there, and that's all you need. It radiates from the hands, just as you expected. And those hands are pulling back the blanket.

It is time to show your teeth.

Boys with Baskets

Somehow Hetsbi and Cade ended up guarding the baskets. Hetsbi wasn't sure how it had happened, but they were told to stand next to Drum and Toppi's father, Maddux, with the baskets at their feet, and they did what they were told. A dead pahaalusk, its shell cracked and dull, sat motionless between the two men, and Hetsbi couldn't take his eyes off it, but when he did, he noticed piles of stones nearby, gathered neatly for an unknown purpose. All the boys and men of the village were there, facing them and waiting for the announcement they knew was coming. It was a sea of dark skin, darker hair, and narrowed eyes, all murmuring and shifting.

"My fellow men," Maddux said. The crowd quieted. "After the death of our menyoro, Drum and I shared the same thought. Each of us wished to humble ourselves and take the menyoro's place."

Drum snorted but didn't interrupt.

"But we could not agree on an arrangement," said Maddux. "So we've come to you."

The assembled men turned to one another, asking questions in a steady thrum: "What is this about?" "Why have they come to us?" "What answers could we possibly have?"

"As I see it, we must work *together* to rebuild our lives and land," Maddux continued. "We must shape our collective knowledge into one mighty force. A village-wide effort, in which your strengths can overcome your neighbor's weaknesses, and the other way around."

No one knew what to say. They'd never heard of such a thing.

Hetsbi's heart thundered. He felt exposed up there,

in the front, and didn't know what his role was. He didn't *want* a role. What would he be asked to do? He felt every dark eye on him, even though he knew they were fixated on Maddux and Drum, trying to work out what was happening, just as he was.

"Imagine if we had an excess of food every year and did not have to trade with the north," Maddux continued.

A voice rose from the crowd: "But we've never succeeded in traveling to the north! Our men disappear at sea!"

"Maybe it's time to end Sailing Day," Maddux suggested.

Drum now spoke: "End Sailing Day? Admit defeat?"

"It's not defeat," Maddux said, over mixed cries of dissent and agreement. "It's using our resources where they're most needed."

Drum scanned the assembly. "I would never cower in the face of challenge."

The crowd found its energy now, an angry energy.

"Listen, men! Listen!" Maddux said, his voice

climbing upward and his hands in the air. "We won't need Sailing Days if we chart a new course!"

"How?" someone cried.

"We will figure it out, together!" proclaimed Maddux.

The noise swelled until Drum stepped forward and climbed atop the pahaalusk shell. How towering he looked, like a giant. Hetsbi's stomach turned. He suddenly felt very small, like one of the stones gathered in the mysterious towers in front of them.

"Maddux is wrong," Drum said. The crowd quieted. "Collective work means collective ruin. There must be one person to lead the village—a man who will demand obedience, skill, and achievement from all people. Even the women. You will do these things because you will be held accountable to me and my son. You will wake up each dawn with a sense of fear and accountability. That is how you build a strong community." Drum turned to Maddux and pointed a thick finger at him. "This man wants you to lower yourself to the ways of women. Cooperation? Bah! I'll not force you to your knees." He turned to the crowd again. "I will force you to rise."

At this, some of the men nodded and clapped. Others were unmoved, still confused. But all eyes were forward, waiting to hear what would come next.

The process would be simple, Maddux said. Each man would take a small rock and place it in one of two baskets. Hetsbi's basket represented a vote for Drum. Cade's basket represented a vote for Maddux. Once all the men had cast their stones, each one would be counted. The count would happen in front of the crowd to prevent dishonesty. Hetsbi and Cade would make sure no one cheated.

The boys and men did as they were told. For the next hour there was no sound except for the *clack, clack, clack* of rock against rock as each man cast his vote.

Hetsbi's basket started to fill. He imagined Drum hovering over him, demanding he get up and serve his purpose. What would a man like that do with a boy like him?

Drum and Maddux observed the casting of stones

quietly. Drum crossed his meaty arms across his chest and stood like a massive pillar, with Kul behind him. Maddux's face was slack and observant.

Clack, clack, went the stones.

Taiting, the boys' teacher, was the last to vote. He placed a rock in Cade's basket.

"Now we count the stones," said Maddux. "Thank you, men, for—"

"We aren't finished!" Drum boomed. He pointed at Hetsbi and Cade. "These two have not yet cast their stones."

Drum pulled two small stones from his own pocket and shoved one at Hetsbi and one at Cade.

Cade didn't hesitate. His stone went to Maddux. *Clack.*

Hetsbi felt like he was swallowing the stone instead of holding it. It might as well have been a boulder.

"Well?" Drum said.

All eyes were on Hetsbi.

It felt that way, at least.

Cade's basket was only three steps away.

But Hetsbi couldn't move.

Those eyes. Drum's eyes.

He dropped the rock into the basket at his feet.

Clack.

Little One

Lalani walked at a cautious pace at first. Then faster. Her feet ached, and she was hungry. It seemed as if this had always been her life—tired feet, hungry body—even though she knew that wasn't true. It only felt that way because the hunger pangs were so palpable. Her stomach knotted and growled. She quickened her step. Faster, faster. Nearer to the injured animal, whose cries came from nowhere and everywhere at the same time.

Her movements became second nature and soon she was taking each step for granted, until her foot landed on some wet leaves and she slipped. Her right leg straightened as she bent her left and instinctively threw the palms of her hands down to soften the fall, which happened with such momentum that it sent a sharp pain through her arms, and then she was sliding, although she wasn't sure how because she didn't remember a hill. But this *was* a hill, because she was going down, reaching out for something to stop the tumble, but finding nothing.

When she finally came to a stop, her feet and calves were scratched and bloody, and all the air had escaped her body. The sky was gray, as if night was coming, although Lalani couldn't actually remember seeing a sun, and how could the sun set if it didn't exist? Shadows fell around her.

She stood, slowly, and brushed herself off. Her wounds stung, but there was no serious damage. No broken bones.

"Usoa?" she called.

Perhaps Usoa had abandoned her.

There was no answer, but there *was* a whimpering.

Lalani turned and saw the animal. It was swaddled in a white blanket.

She looked around, not sure what she expected to see. Maybe its mother, ready to defend her young. But there was nothing.

The creature squirmed. A nose poked up. Whiskers. Two round eyes, cream-colored fur.

It was a wallecta. The blanket wiggled as it struggled to break free.

Lalani heard Drum. She heard Kul.

You're as useless as a wallecta.

"Don't worry, little one," Lalani said. "I'm here."

The Animal That Never Was

Lalani realized there was no wallecta the moment she pulled back the blanket. A shriek sliced the air—it came from the blanket, from the creature *inside* the blanket, a creature of red mist and sharp teeth. Lalani shielded her face and this *thing* pierced her skin and gnawed the soft tendons of her thumb. Her eyes flooded with vapor. Her ears flooded with screeching. She fell back and kicked. She reached for Ellseth's pouch with her other hand and fumbled for the arrowhead.

The arrowhead wasn't much of a weapon, but the thing wailed when she stabbed it, so she did it again and again and again. She didn't have time to consider what she was doing, but somehow, with her small shaky hand and her small makeshift weapon, she was fighting, and she fought until something lifted her up and she was floating.

How was she floating? She was above the ground and something was carrying her. Something with rough edges and rustling hair. Hard, but gentle to the touch.

This something reached out and fought for her.

She looked up. She saw nothing but leaves.

She was being lifted by a tree.

Yes, this was a mighty branch cradling her like a baby. Creating a green canopy of protection around her and fighting with its branches.

The misty thing was weakening. Sputtering. Sparking bits of fire. It was breaking apart, but still trying desperately to get to Lalani and her hands.

She looked at them now. They were red and swollen, but no blood.

She was jostled back and forth as the tree threw its weight around.

The thing whimpered a final time.

The beautiful tree rustled its leaves.

Shh, it said to Lalani. *Shh*.

Three Days Left

Lalani didn't know how long she slept, but her body screamed with pain when she opened her eyes. Her lids were heavy, as if she'd slept for a thousand years.

A voice slipped into her consciousness.

"Lalani? Are you okay?"

Usoa.

Am I? Lalani breathed deeply. She smelled something sweet and vaguely familiar and turned her head—a pyramid of carefully placed osabana.

The light had changed. It was either dusk or dawn, she couldn't tell which. A complicated knot of meha branches towered above her. When she sat up, carefully and painfully, Usoa placed an osabana in her hand.

"How long have I been asleep?" Lalani asked. "How did you find me?"

"I don't know how long you've been asleep," said Usoa. She was sitting on the ground next to Lalani, with her horns resting against the tree. "You were asleep when I found you, hours ago. When you didn't come back, I searched and searched. When I heard the yootah, I thought for sure it got you. But then I found you here, with the osabana again. I thought you were dead, but then I noticed you were breathing." She cocked her head to one side. "How did you do it?"

"Do what?" Lalani stretched her back. Oh, how she ached.

"Make it out alive."

Lalani tried to remember what had happened. She'd used the arrowhead, hadn't she? "I think . . . the tree . . ."

Usoa nodded, as if she needed no further explanation.

Lalani peeled the osabana clumsily. "Where is all this food coming from?"

"It was here when I found you, just like last time."

Lalani stopped peeling and looked at her hands. The swelling was gone.

"The tree saved me from that thing. Do you think it gathered this fruit, too?"

Usoa raised a single eyebrow. "A tree can't do that."

"Then who?"

"I don't know. Maybe it's best not to question too much and simply say 'thank you.'"

Lalani took another bite and turned her eyes toward the sky. *Thank you.*

Brother, Sister

Veyda found Hetsbi sitting near the rock bed where the Oragleo sisters had claimed to have discovered Ziva's hair. His eyes were set on the horizon.

"What are you looking at out there?" Veyda asked.

"Nothing."

So Veyda joined him and looked at nothing, too.

"What are you thinking about?" Veyda asked.

"Nothing." After a long silence, Hetsbi said, "You don't seem upset. I don't understand why."

"What do you mean?"

"Lalani. She's . . ." his voice cracked ". . . gone."

Veyda thought of Lalani standing in the darkness, asking for a promise. "Things aren't that simple, Hetsbi." She pulled her hair over her shoulder and braided it absently. "Anyway, I don't think she's really gone."

Hetsbi narrowed his eyes. "What do you mean?"

"She didn't die in the landslide. I know for sure. I saw her after." Veyda was unsure if she should continue. Hetsbi was trustworthy, but Lalani's visit felt like a secret.

"Saw her? Where?"

"She came to our house in the middle of the night. She said she had to go somewhere, and asked me to look after her mother. Then she left." Veyda paused. "That's all I know."

Hetsbi nibbled his bottom lip. His face morphed into a knot of concern.

"Where do you think she was going?" Hetsbi asked. "Why would she leave?"

Veyda unbraided. Braided again. "I don't know."

"Do you think she was going back to the mountain?"

"No." She wasn't—was she? "No one would be able to get up there now. What's left of it, anyway."

Hetsbi's eyes glistened. "Maybe she went north. Maybe she found an abandoned ship and set sail." A tear balanced on the rim of his eyelash. "Maybe she's on top of Mount Isa right now, with all of life's fortunes at her feet."

"Yes. And maybe . . ." Veyda gathered her thoughts. She made medicine. She was no storyteller. ". . . and maybe she's going to load all those fortunes onto the ship in the morning and come back for us."

That's when Hetsbi's tear fell. And then she cried, too. Because they knew it was a ridiculous idea, someone like Lalani sailing across the distant sea.

Here is what Hetsbi was really thinking when Veyda found him looking at nothing:

I am a coward.

This was the mantra that ran through his mind. He thought of how he'd kept quiet when Cade needed him to speak up. He thought of the sound his stone made when it dropped into Drum's basket.

Clack. The sound rang in his head as he and Veyda walked home. *Clack.* It echoed as he helped Veyda care for Lalani's mother. *Clack*, as he told his own mother good night. It wasn't until he climbed into his corner of the sleeping room that he gathered the words to ask Veyda whom she would have voted for.

"Drum or Maddux?" whispered Hetsbi, because everyone else was asleep by then.

"Maddux, of course." She turned to him in the darkness. "Why?"

But Hetsbi didn't answer. The words "of course" rang silently in the darkness.

When he closed his eyes to sleep, he heard it again.

Clack.

Clack.

Clack.

YOU ARE BAI—VINCA

Imagine you are a majestic bird. Nine feet tall with a curved beak made of the sharpest keratin. You wake each morning in a hollow tree—the biggest in the forest, large enough for you and your sister. When you emerge, it's as if the tree has come to life.

You settle your heavy claws in the earth and stretch your wings as your sister sleeps in her nest. Your wings are so broad and powerful that the leaves flutter when you move them. This makes you very proud. There is no other creature with broad and powerful wings such as these. Except for your family, of course. You think of them as you study the brilliant colors of your feathers. Your family prefers to sleep past dawn, but you are an early bird.

You take in the world with your astonishing eyes. You see colors of every shade and hue, all the complicated patterns of the leaves, and every ridge in the tree trunks, like stagnant waterfalls. You study as much as you can in the peace of the morning because your eyesight is sharp and clear, and you are proud of this, too.

You see a collection of pachenka nuts and make the short journey toward them. You rely on pachenka. Your species is called the bai, and the bai are the only living beings that can eat pachenka, because only the bai can crack them open. It's as if the pachenka's thick, hardened shell was designed specifically for your beak.

You eat other things, too. Mostly berries. Sometimes you grow weary of pachenka, but you cannot live without them. They are packed with rich clusters of protein and nutrients that keep the bai healthy. Your home in the hollow tree is in the middle of a grove of pachenka trees, which produce food at a tremendous rate. There is always plenty. You are never hungry.

You can carry three pachenka in your beak at one time, and every morning you select the best ones. Two for your sister and one for yourself. She will insist that you eat the third one, but you will insist just the same, and eventually she will relent. Your heart swells with joy when your sister gets the last bite; it's better than having it for yourself.

You gather a cluster of wild berries before you leave. Your sister loves berries, especially the red ones.

This is your routine. Today is the same as yesterday—or is it? You fly home with your spoils, unaware that your eyes have missed something. They are sharp and accurate and see clearly, but only if you're paying attention. So you don't notice the blight on the pachenka tree. The blister is smaller than your pupil. It is hidden in plain sight. But you have always been surrounded by the pachenka trees. They have always produced food. They have never been ill a day in their lives. You don't know to look for such things.

Nevertheless, it is there.

It's amazing how something smaller than a pupil can turn deadly, isn't it? You should never underestimate the power of small things in great numbers. The blister, the blight, started small, but it grew and grew. That's what happens when no one is paying attention. Eventually the tiny issue became a momentous problem—big enough to take down the bai. You didn't see it coming. You didn't think anything could threaten the bai. Look how mighty you are, after all. Look at those broad wings and that glorious beak! And don't forget about the talons. Your beautiful, frightening claws. You'd never known fear. Why would you? You certainly never knew to fear the pachenka nuts that nourished the bai for generations.

Your sister got sick. She was so ill that she could

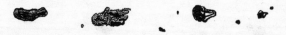

not lift her wings. The other bai knew what was coming, and they urged you to fly away with them. They were going to settle somewhere else. A place where the pachenka trees were not diseased. By this time, there was only one healthy tree remaining, and that wasn't enough to feed all of you. You knew this. You're no fool. But how could you leave your sister?

"Go without me," you said to the others. "I'll find you."

You never gave it a second thought. You couldn't let your sister die alone. Your fellow bai didn't argue with you; they knew better. So they all flew away, like a great thunderstorm passing over. You weren't prepared for how quiet the world would become without them.

Soon your sister no longer knew you. She could hardly open her eyes. You sang to her, even though she'd always said you had no voice for singing. You nuzzled your beak into the soft dampness of her feathers. You covered her with your wings. You only left when you had to, when you became so hungry that you needed to eat. There were times when you considered eating from the poisoned trees—how could you live without your sister?—but you knew better. Your sister would die, yes, and it would be painful, but you'd made a promise to find your fellow bai. You would all nurse your sorrows together. So you ate from the only untainted pachenka tree that remained.

It happened, but not the way you expected.

While you searched for food and your sister lay dying, an outsider invaded the grove. A thief. Your sister was too weak to fight when he hacked away her talon. When you came back, she was already dead.

You wept for hours.

She was gone now, and you were all alone.

But not for long.

You gave your sister's body to the sea, just as she would have wanted, and flew off to join your fellow bai. You longed for their company. You needed to share your sorrow. Sadness becomes poison if you let it sit too long. Once you found your flock, you would empty your sadness upon them, and they would do the same, and together you would find strength to continue your new life, in this new place, wherever it was.

The bai are mighty.

The bai are majestic.

Too mighty and majestic to go unnoticed.

It never occurred to you that you might never find them.

Other things occurred to you, though. Like the extra time you could have spent with your sister, if she had not bled to death. Those moments were stolen. If this merciless thief wanted talons so badly, you had plenty of your own to offer, and you had time to wait. When bai are healthy, their lives are long—and so is their memory.

A Death on the Horizon

Usoa led Lalani to a stream where they drank huge handfuls of water. The osabana was adequate at quenching Lalani's hunger, but it didn't last forever. Usoa didn't seem to need much sustenance. She could go for long stretches without drinking, and if she became hungry, she simply pulled a stalk of grass out of the ground and ate it.

The water was so clean that it sparkled, and Lalani was grateful, although it reminded her of the creek by Ellseth's house. Anytime she recalled Ellseth, a wave of nausea washed through her. She'd noticed more feelings like this, actually—a swishing belly, throbbing headache, and strange thoughts that didn't make much sense. There was a moment, a fleeting moment, when she confused Usoa for Veyda.

They sat on the bank of the stream with water dripping from their chins. They were in another bright swath of forest, so Lalani kept an eye out for ebee and balawuk. She counted the mounds within view. One, two, three, four, five.

From this vantage point, the island looked peaceful again. It didn't seem like a place where screeching things attacked your hands or trees ate the spirits of the dead. It didn't seem like a place where peaceful mindoren were killed by vicious creatures.

Lalani picked up a tiny pebble and tossed it into the water.

"I'm sorry about your mother," she said.

Usoa had her legs stretched out in front of her, strong like tree trunks. She didn't say anything.

"My father died, too," Lalani continued. "And now my mother—" Lalani closed her eyes. Her head thundered. She thought of her mother. Her face. Her hands when she mended. "She's dying."

"Is someone with her?" asked Usoa.

Whoosh-whoosh. Lalani couldn't answer. She heard her heartbeat in her ears.

"I want to tell you a secret," Usoa said, when Lalani didn't say anything.

The words jumbled together inside Lalani's headache. She tried to pick them apart, place them in the right order, and make sense of them. But she suddenly felt very ill.

There is a death on the horizon.

Was Usoa still talking, or was she imagining it?

I'm going to kill Bai-Vinca.

I didn't even bring a weapon.

I want to kill her with my bare hands.

Whoosh-whoosh.

Are you okay, Lalani?

Lie down for a moment.

Shh. Shh. It's okay.

It's because of the goyuk.

That's another reason I wanted to come with you.

Are you sleeping now?

Good.

Shh. Shh.

I'm sorry about the goyuk. I didn't think it was fair to tell you everything.

Nothing can be done about it. So I saw no need to alarm you.

I'm here, though. And I'm happy I'm here.

No one should die alone.

Gong

Say what you will about Drum, but he was a man who kept his promises. After the stones were counted in his favor, he promised to rule with fear, and he did. He erected a gong near the central water pump, and Kul struck it each morning at dawn with a heavy gavel that sent a vibrating call through the village. *GONNNNNGG. GONNNNNGG.* Drum would appear then, his back straight and proud, a smile plastered on his face; he looked like he'd just killed someone and gotten away with it.

The *GONNNNNGG* was meant to wake the villagers

up, and it worked. They rolled out of their beds and opened their eyes. The next sound they heard was Drum. His voice was much like the gong.

He commanded them to wake up.

He reminded them of their duties.

He told them that they would be judged.

He would watch with a careful eye, and if you faltered, he'd put you in your proper place, just as he'd done with Lalani and the basin.

But after Drum's morning announcements, the village quieted and the echoes of the gong faded, mixing into the ordinary sounds of Sanlagita.

But Hetsbi heard things others did not.

Clack.

He had failed as a fisherman.

Clack.

He had failed as a shipbuilder.

Clack.

He had failed his conscience.

Clack. Clack.

These thoughts circled and circled in his mind. They followed him to school, where Taiting pretended it was business as usual, but Hetsbi wondered: Was Taiting judging him or had he imagined it? Did all the boys know he had cast a stone out of fear? How had the others voted?

When the *clacks* became too much, Hetsbi decided to find out.

A Simple Solution

Taiting had many students, but Hetsbi had only one teacher, so Hetsbi had time and space to collect observations and come to conclusions about what kind of man Taiting was. It hadn't taken long for Hetsbi to discover that his teacher was a man of integrity and honor. He was fair and just. He preferred not to show favoritism. He tempered criticism with encouragement. He did not use physical intimidation like Drum; there was nothing to fear about him. Did that make Taiting weak? Hetsbi had struggled with this question before the landslide, but now he knew the answer. Taiting had cast his stone for

Maddux, and no weak man could do such a thing.

Hetsbi waited for Cade and the other boys to disappear down the dirt road to the village, then he walked around the building, where Taiting was gathering wood.

"Taiting?" said Hetsbi.

Taiting lifted his head over his armful of branches. His face relaxed into a smile. "Hetsbi. Can I help you with something?"

Hetsbi nibbled his bottom lip.

"Maybe," he said. Unfortunately, he hadn't considered the details. How do you start such a conversation? How do you ask someone to make you a better man?

Taiting placed the branches onto a carefully stacked pile nearby. Stray branches were everywhere since the landslide. It occurred to Hetsbi that he should help his teacher, but he was too nervous to move or offer.

Instead, he blurted out: "Why did the menyoro select you to become a teacher?"

"Well," Taiting said, brushing his hands. "I suppose I wasn't good at anything else."

"You weren't good at fishing?"

"Not particularly."

"Or shipbuilding?"

"I know enough of both to start instruction and recognize others who excel at it. I can catch fish and build a boat, but it won't be the most fish or the best boat." He brought his arms up, then dropped them to his sides, as if to say *that is that.* "I suppose the menyoro chose me to teach because I have hope in abundance."

"Hope for what?"

"That my students will become better."

Hetsbi looked away. "What if they don't?"

"Is there something you want to discuss with me, Hetsbi? Is there something I can help you with?"

Hetsbi thought of Cade, walking so confidently. The way he expertly baited his fishing hooks and sanded his scouting boat. The way he stood up for Lalani when Hetsbi couldn't be bothered.

Why couldn't everyone get equal doses of confidence to go around?

"I cast my stone for Drum," said Hetsbi.

"Yes."

Hetsbi swallowed. "Do you think badly of me?"

"Of course not. Each man had the right to cast his stone however he chose. I would never expect my students to do everything as I do, or to believe the things that I believe."

"But . . ." Hetsbi began. "But what if they *do* believe the things you believe?"

"I'm not sure I understand."

"I didn't want to cast my stone that way," Hetsbi said. Almost a whisper.

"I see."

"I was a coward," Hetsbi said.

He raised his eyes to his teacher.

"We have many opportunities in life to overcome fear and embrace courage," said Taiting. "Once we seize the first opportunity, it becomes easier to seize the second." He paused. "But you are not a coward, Hetsbi. I know this to be true."

"How do you know?" he asked.

"If you were a coward, you wouldn't be standing here," said Taiting. "Living what you believe can be just as difficult as living in silence. Sometimes even more so."

The words were coming easier to Hetsbi now. "I'm tired of thinking myself a coward."

"Then there is a simple solution," Taiting said.

"What is it?"

"Seize the next opportunity, of course," said Taiting.

Bai-Vinca

The bird came from nowhere. One moment Lalani was trying to avoid the mounds—they were everywhere now—and quiet the whooshing in her head and the next, a tremendous noise pierced the forest. *SQUAWW SQUAWW SQUAWW.* Usoa clutched Lalani's elbow.

"That's her," she said.

Lalani followed Usoa's gaze, squinting into a slant of light. Something moved. Glided, really. Huge wings cast an enormous shadow.

Usoa balled her hands into fists and put them on her hips.

Lalani's hair blew in all directions. Leaves lifted and swirled from the ground. Bai-Vinca brought a scent with her. Sweet and earthy. *Why aren't we running?* Lalani thought. Her feet itched. *Run, run,* they said. But Usoa didn't move, so neither did she.

The creature landed in front of them more delicately than Lalani would have imagined. Lalani might have said that Bai-Vinca was beautiful, with brilliantly colored feathers of yellow, red, green, and blue. But her eyes, talons, and beak—also sharp, very sharp indeed—made her terrifying.

Bai-Vinca towered over Lalani and Usoa. She could easily engulf them with her wings. Her eyes were bigger than Lalani's hands and they were in constant motion, flitting and blinking.

"What are you doing on the bai's land?" Bai-Vinca said. Her words sounded diced or chopped as she maneuvered her strange, thick tongue around her beaked mouth.

"This land no longer belongs to the bai," said Usoa. "There are no bai. Only you."

Bai-Vinca's gaze fell on Lalani. "What are you?"

"She's human," Usoa replied. "From another place."

"Another place," Bai-Vinca repeated, her eyes softening. She ruffled her feathers. "Do you bring word about my family?"

Lalani didn't know what to say. Was this a trick question?

"No one will ever bring word about your family," Usoa answered.

Bai-Vinca's enormous eyes darted toward her.

"But I bring word of mine," Usoa continued.

Usoa swung a tight fist into Bai-Vinca's eye, which gleamed like a target, and Bai-Vinca squawked so loudly that Lalani pressed her hands to her ears because the squawking made her head throb so, so badly—it was loud, much too loud—and Bai-Vinca stumbled back, a flurry of color, startled yet again when Usoa kicked her once, twice, three times, but by the fourth swift kick, Bai-Vinca was ready. She spread her wings and it was such a stunning sight that Usoa froze, speechless, and that single moment was all it took. Bai-Vinca raised herself off the ground, hovering, hovering, then threw her feet out and sank her talons into Usoa's shoulder. Usoa screamed—a mighty, mighty scream.

"Let her go!" Lalani cried, released at last from her cowering place. She wrapped both hands around Bai-Vinca's leathery ankles and pulled. "Let her go! Let her go!"

Usoa and Lalani were both on the ground now. A tree root pushed into Lalani's back as she and Usoa kicked and screamed and wailed, and when something warm and wet rushed over Lalani's hands, she realized that it was Usoa's blood and this made her fight even more fiercely. Bai-Vinca tried to snatch Lalani, but Lalani was small and quick and rolled out of the way, catching dirt in her mouth. She fumbled for the pouch around her neck, searching for the arrowhead, but she wasn't able to latch onto it as Bai-Vinca aimed her beak at them. She pecked, pecked, pecked the earth around their heads. Her beak cut the dirt. It sliced Lalani's cheek and ear. But Bai-Vinca's throat was exposed, a soft and delicate gullet where Lalani sank her teeth and Usoa followed her lead. The girls punched and bit and kicked, and soon Bai-Vinca's squawks devolved into choked cries as they overpowered her. Bai-Vinca brought her wings back, then pumped them forward in two powerful flaps. The momentum broke the three of them apart. Usoa and Lalani crumpled to the ground in a heap and Bai-Vinca flew up, but not away.

Blood. Everywhere. Lalani pressed her hands against Usoa's shoulder. Veyda had once told her that you should put pressure on a bleeding wound to stop the gushing, and that's just what she did as Bai-Vinca hovered over them. Her wings were so vast that their force rustled their hair, and she was so large and mighty that Lalani felt herself shrinking, and when the talons came charging down again, Lalani rolled out of the way, because when you are small and don't take up much space, it can be easier to move from here to there, and sometimes moving from here to there is all you need to do to save yourself.

Bai-Vinca's talons sank into the earth instead of

Lalani, and both girls darted out of the way in the seconds
it took for Bai-Vinca to pull them out again.

Lalani ran. When she zigzagged, Bai-Vinca had
trouble keeping up with her. It was tricky for Bai-Vinca
to fly this close to the ground, so she glided up, up, up,
for a better view. When Lalani saw a big tree with a
narrow hollow in the trunk, she raced to it and wiggled
her way in. The hole was large enough for Usoa, too, but
she barely made it through the opening because of her
horns. The girls pushed themselves as far back as they
could.

Bai-Vinca squawked and landed in front of the tree,
blocking the light. The little space, which smelled like
wet leaves and damp grass, darkened. Usoa's clipped
breathing tangled with the whooshing in Lalani's head.

Bai-Vinca peered in at them with one colossal eye.

"You can't survive in there forever," Bai-Vinca said.

Lalani took stock of what they had to defend
themselves with, and it wasn't much. One human girl,
one injured mindoren girl. Four arms, four hands, four

legs, four feet, two horns. One small arrowhead.

Just as Lalani thought *it's not enough*, Usoa started yanking and pulling at something overhead. *Snap, snap.* A piece of the bark broke off; she held it like a weapon.

Then she used it like one.

She burst from the tree and ran the sharp end through Bai-Vinca's belly. Oh, how the creature shrieked. Bai-Vinca staggered backward. Her chest heaved. Blue sprays of blood splashed the tree, splattering Usoa's and Lalani's faces. Bai-Vinca lifted one wing then the other. She opened her beak wide. Lalani pressed her hands against her ears, ready for the piercing wail. Her hands were wet with blood. But instead of screaming, Bai-Vinca whispered, "Do you have word about my family?"

Then, like a great mountain cleaving in half, she fell.

Bai-Vinca didn't die right away, but it was clear to Usoa and Lalani that her death was a certainty. Usoa sputtered and moaned, her back against the tree, her face dotted with Bai-Vinca's blue blood.

"I need to get help," Lalani said.

"The only creatures here are the nunso," whispered Usoa. Her eyes were barely open now. "Besides, you're running out of time."

"Time for what?" Lalani asked, back to pressing her hands against Usoa's wound as hard as she could.

"Tell me a story."

"A story? I don't understand . . ."

"Something to make me cry," said Usoa. "There isn't time. Please."

Lalani took Usoa's hand. She didn't understand what was happening. This was such a strange place full of strange riddles—Bai-Vinca and her family; trees that spoke, saved, and offered salvation; and now, a story to make a dying mindoren cry.

Lalani's Story

Anya of Arkaley was cursed. It was clear from the moment she was born. She looked like no other infant in the village. Although Anya had two hands, two feet, ten fingers, and ten toes, she had an oddity that no one in Arkaley had ever seen: a small shell. It was on her back. It stretched from her waist to her neck. And there was nothing to be done. The leader of Arkaley told the villagers to avoid Anya at all costs or risk being cursed themselves. To make matters worse, it kept getting bigger. It grew, just like her hair or her fingernails. By the time she was thirteen years old, you could no longer see her back at all. Just the shell. And it was heavy, too. Anya grew weary from carrying all that weight. And her heart grew weary, too, because she had no friends. The other children didn't understand why she had this shell. It must have been something she'd done, they said. She must be wicked or diseased, they said. It was rumored that if you touched her shell, you would die—though this wasn't true. Even Anya's parents were ashamed of her. What had they done to deserve such an absurd child? Didn't they have enough to worry over?

What do you think Anya's shell looked like? Don't think of it as anything beautiful. It was ragged and lumpy, and there were no brilliant shades of red, blue, or green. Think of the color of dust. Think of the bark of a dead tree. This was Anya's shell.

Poor Anya. You can imagine how desperately she wished for her shell to disappear. Every night she fell asleep and wished for her burden to wither away and die. She prayed that she would wake up surrounded by broken pieces, free. But that never happened.

Time did nothing to comfort Anya. But she never gave up hope that she would be like everyone else one day. She did everything she could to rid herself of that shell. She banged it against the biggest tree in the village. She begged a huntsman to hack it off. She tried to burn it, even. But it was stubborn and sturdy and part of her, so nothing worked. By the time she was twenty, Anya no longer believed in miracles, but then a miracle appeared. A traveler. A man named Zo Zi.

The people of Arkaley had never seen a foreigner, especially one like Zo Zi. He told them he traveled the world and collected things along the way. One of the things he collected was knowledge, and he offered it to everyone, including Anya. He told her that he could remove her shell for a price, and she promised to give him everything she owned. It wasn't much. Her parents had died and left behind a small house, but she gladly offered it to Zo Zi. She said she would return to the village as a normal woman, and she would find a new home. Maybe a man would ask for her hand in marriage. Could you imagine?

Zo Zi put her in a deep, deep sleep. When she awoke, Zo Zi was gone, but he had kept his promise. Her shell lay intact beside her. She looked like everyone else, even if she didn't understand her new body. She fell over when she walked. But soon, with practice, she carried herself like an everyday Arkaley woman. Her hair brushed the skin between her shoulder blades. It tickled and delighted her. How surprised the town would be! She imagined their faces. The men rushing to marry her, the women rushing to be her friend.

Anya had nowhere to put her shell. Zo Zi was a man of his word. Every beam of her home was gone and sold. Only a charred pit remained—the place where the hearth had once been.

Anya found a place to stow the shell so she could walk through Arkaley without it. She couldn't wait for everyone to see her! The *real* her.

But when she arrived, the people of Arkaley didn't greet her with hugs and hellos. They regarded her as they always did—faces full of shock and disgust.

What happened to your shell? they asked, their mouths puckered in disapproval.

I had it removed, she replied.

The villagers scurried away, frightened by this new Anya. She'd become even more foreign to them than before. Each person she met was afraid. The only thing she heard was *Why? Why? Why did you remove your shell?* And hidden underneath this was another clear, unspoken question: *Why did you think you could be one of us?*

They threw her out of the village. It took two men to hoist her shell through the gate. They called her a freak. An animal without a herd.

"I am a person, and I am here!" cried Anya. She pounded her fists on the gates. Without her shell to weigh her down, she had more power than before. "I am here! I am here!"

Only one person answered. A man with a heavy voice. "Not anymore," he yelled.

Anya carried her shell to the next town. What else could she do? But the people there refused to open their gates.

By the time she'd reached the fourth town, her body was bruised and weak. She was hungry and thirsty. She still carried her shell. Why? She didn't know. What was the point? No one wanted it. The shell served no purpose. So she climbed a cliff and threw it off. She watched it plummet to the rocky shore and crack in three pieces, and she'd never felt so triumphant or defiant in her life. As if the shell had its own mind and had dared her to conquer it, which she had. Anya stood on the cliff and thought of going over, too. Instead, she left the broken shell behind and walked ten miles to the next village. It looked much like all the others. She knocked lightly at the gates and asked to be let in. Did they have room for one more? She was lost and lonely, and needed food and water.

But this village was quite different. When the guard opened the gate, Anya saw that the people here had shells!

Her heart leaped. She could have wept with joy.

"My herd!" she cried. "Finally, I have found my herd!"

But the guard looked at her coldly and asked who

she was and where she was from. She explained. She told him about the shell and Zo Zi. The man studied her from head to toe.

"If you're one of us, show me your shell. Then you may enter," he said. "You can live a life of luxury and riches. All will welcome you. You will be loved and adored for everything you are, and you will never worry again. But first you must show me the shell."

Anya said, "I threw it off a cliff, and it cracked in three pieces."

The man's face tightened with horror. "Why would you do such a thing? That shell was part of you. It was meant to be revered and celebrated."

"The villagers ridiculed me! They would not accept me with a shell," Anya pleaded.

"Rather than adore your shell, you sought the love of those who ridiculed you." The man shook his head. "This is a great tragedy."

He closed the gate. He didn't slam it or kick it shut. He closed it quietly, which made it worse somehow.

Anya no longer had the energy to cry or scream or fight. She'd finally found the place where she belonged, and now she didn't belong anywhere. She had nothing to protect her and no one to keep her company. No herd. No shell.

"I am here," she said, one last time, to remind herself.

But she no longer believed it.

Cade

Cade Malay had a secret. For years, even before he was old enough to go to school, he enjoyed sneaking out of his house at night and walking to the northern shore. It was a journey of several miles each way, but it passed quickly because he knew the steps by heart. Quick as a wallecta, he scurried down all the correct paths and by all the right trees until he was sitting alone, staring into the mist.

Cade knew what kind of boy he was. The kind who wore his ax-saw around his waist, wasn't afraid to cast his stone in the right basket, and helped his friends with their hooks and scouting boats if he finished his own projects early. Most of the time Cade didn't pass many hours considering how he felt about all these things or what sort of person he wanted to become. Cade was Cade.

Or so he thought.

Ever since his brother had sailed off and Lalani had disappeared, something had changed. He was still the same boy, but it was no longer enough. Maybe it was because of Drum. The way Drum pounded his heavy gavel against the gong and demanded that the people do more, more, more. The way he chastised the men and women, boys and girls, when they didn't achieve his standards. Cade wondered how he had treated Lalani. How he would treat the village over the next one year, two years, ten. Sanlagita was hardly a paradise—how much worse would it get with Drum leading the charge?

Staring at the water helped Cade think, even before he knew he had so much to think about. That's why he'd been coming to the shore now more than ever. He'd promised himself and his mother that he would never try to sail across the sea—if the others hadn't survived, why would he?—but like most people of Sanlagita, his mind wandered with possibilities.

If there were people across the sea, were they happy? He hoped so.

Did they know of Sanlagita? He hoped not.

The water also made him think about Lalani. They hadn't talked much, not really, but he missed her. Before Kahna fell, he'd often noticed her with Veyda and Hetsbi, and the sight of her made him nervous. Cade was rarely nervous, so the feeling had confused him at first. He wondered what was behind Lalani's eyes the same way he wondered what was across the water, and so what if his heart jittered when he saw her?

Now the only thing that made him jittery was fear for the future.

Cade sighed. The northern shore scared most people, especially at night, but that's when Cade loved it most. He appreciated its predictability. Night after night, the sea was the same.

Except.

Something was different tonight.

Cade peered into the fog. The change was subtle. If he hadn't stared at this horizon hundreds of times before, he wouldn't have noticed it. But there—not far out—the veil shifted and parted, wisps of mist lifting lazily into the air.

The veil never parted unless a ship was cutting through.

But the ships were always sailing *away* from Sanlagita. This ship—and yes, he saw now that it was indeed a ship—was coming *toward* him.

Cade stood. He put his hand on his ax-saw, but he wasn't scared. Only curious and prepared. He didn't move. He waited for the ship to announce itself. Soon it did. Strangely. It arrived quietly, with barely a lap of the water. Cade was already a skilled scout and shipbuilder and understood the logic of sailing, so he knew right away that there was no one on board. No one alive, anyway.

He also knew that he had seen this ship before.

He knew it well.

In Sanlagita

Here is what happened after Cade saw the ship: he ran and told his mother.

Clusters of men hurried north. Yes, it was Esdel's ship. Abandoned, as if the sailors had never existed. Maybe they'd become part of the fog. How were the villagers to know what happened on that distant sea?

When a mysterious ship washes ashore, it twists your mind with ideas. There were two people in the crowd that day whose minds turned more than most.

One of those people was Drum.

The other was Hetsbi.

Challenge

Drum was relentless with the gong. It echoed through the village and didn't stop until Drum was convinced that everyone had emerged from their houses to hear what he had to say. On this particular morning, he didn't even wait for dawn. The villagers were bleary-eyed and sleepy.

All but Hetsbi, who wanted to be as close to Drum as possible.

By the time the rest of the villagers had gathered around their new menyoro, Hetsbi's feet were planted up front. Veyda joined him. She took his hand and squeezed it once. His heart pounded against his chest. But he kept his shoulders square and his breath steady.

Once everyone was situated and focused on their leader—careful not to look away, since that invited public shaming—Drum and Kul stepped forward. Drum puffed out his chest and announced that Esdel's boat had been found in good condition, but with no living souls on board. He offered passing condolences to Esdel's family—none of whom were there, as far as Hetsbi could tell—but quickly steered the conversation to his grand new idea: he wanted to use the wood from the boat to build a stately home for himself and Kul. He didn't mention his wife, who was still living with Lo Yuzi, but he made sure to remark that the home of the menyoro should have room for "companions and children," despite the tradition that the menyoro remain unmarried and childless to prove his dedication to the villagers.

"I need additional builders," said Drum. "Come forward to volunteer."

The crowd stirred. No one wanted to volunteer. The Sanlagitans were weak and hungry, and volunteering meant working under Drum day after day. It meant taking apart a grand ship that the shipbuilders had built together and reducing it to a single home for one person while the rest of them suffered. They knew Drum and Kul took unfair portions of food already. What more did they want?

Hetsbi shifted his weight from one foot to another.

"Why should we dismantle a perfect ship?" Hetsbi called out, when the crowd was at its quietest, before he lost his nerve.

Hetsbi had meant to appear forceful and commanding, but his voice rose and fell, and sounded like a dying animal. Drum's expression went from impatience to amusement when he realized it was Hetsbi who had dared to speak to him. Kul crossed his arms and narrowed his eyes.

"Excuse me, *boy*," said Drum, turning to face Hetsbi. "What did you say?"

Hetsbi cleared his throat. "We shouldn't dismantle a perfectly good ship!" His voice was steady now. "They take years to build, and this one is ready to sail!"

Kul laughed. "Are *you* offering to captain the ship?"

The silence broke as people chuckled nervously. Hetsbi Yuzi manning a ship? The boy couldn't even catch a fish.

"No," Hetsbi said. "I'm not man enough. Anyone can see that." He paused. "But you are! You're the strongest man in the village! That is why you're our menyoro!"

It was early morning, but now the village was awake. As soon as the words left Hetsbi's mouth, the silence cracked open. The villagers leaned toward each other, talking, their eyes alight with possibility.

His plan was growing wings.

Hetsbi suddenly felt light on his feet.

Drum's face contorted in confusion. "I can't sail, idiot boy. I'm your leader. Without me, your crops would fail. Your nets would be empty. You would all be buried by Kahna, or worse." He glanced toward Kul, who stood tall and still, and snorted half-heartedly. "Don't be stupid."

No one bothered to point out that those things had already happened.

"I know you're our leader," said Hetsbi. "That is why I have faith that you can make the journey. Who else but you? When else but now? There's a perfectly good ship waiting, and no one here is fit to steer it, except for you and your son."

Maddux stepped forward now, breaking away from the crowd. "The boy is right, menyoro. If you're as strong and mighty as you say you are, you wouldn't be afraid. Look at all the men who went before you. Do you believe they're better than you? If you don't sail, that's just how it appears."

Drum strode to Maddux in three giant steps.

"I'm no fool," Drum said. "I won't sail off so *you* can become menyoro. What do you take me for?"

A voice rose up from the back of the crowd: "Hetsbi is right! You are the only man who can save us." It was Cade. He stepped forward with his ax-saw around his waist. He glanced Hetsbi's way, just for a moment.

They now had a shared understanding.

"My brother failed," Cade said. "But you can succeed. I know that now. I've seen you work in the village. You're the only one. You and Kul."

"Do it for us!" Caralita, one of the washerwomen, cried.

"Do it for us!" someone else shouted. Taiting?

Another voice then another. Over and over. "Do it for us! Do it for us!"

As the crowd grew louder and louder, Drum lifted his thick hands to quiet them. It took a long while for the cheers to settle down.

"I understand your belief in me, but I will not leave my position as menyoro. Not when there's a fool who is set to take my place," Drum said, nodding toward Maddux. "Besides, I am trained as a fisherman, not a sailor."

"If you're afraid," Cade said, his voice low. "Admit it."

Drum narrowed his eyes. "Afraid?"

"Do it for us, menyoro!" Hetsbi cried. He launched into a chant: "For us! For us!"

Veyda was the first to join him. Soon, though, the chant moved like a fever through the crowd and within seconds, the villagers were bouncing on their feet and pumping their fists, nervous with excitement under the now-rising sun.

YOU ARE ZIVA

Imagine you are a ghost. You have no today. You have no tomorrow. You have only yesterday. And many yesterdays ago, you were a girl—flesh and blood, walking the earth, full of wishes and dreams, just like anyone. You weren't prideful. You weren't beautiful. Quite the opposite. But you cherished your hair. When times were difficult (and they often were), you twisted it around your fingers and reminded yourself that you were alive and breathing and the world had much to offer, if you could find it.

You tried. Oh, how you tried. But you had no choices, no options. You had no school. You had no skills, other than mending and pulling vegetables. It had been that way for generations before you, and it would be that way for generations after.

So you took your chance. You waited for a Sailing Day and stowed yourself away.

You planned to announce yourself once the ship was far from Sanlagita, and that's just what you did. You stepped out of the belly of the boat and told the men you were there. They were furious, as you knew they would be, but what could they do? They wouldn't throw you overboard.

You were right.

For a time.

The fog confused them. They forgot their names. They forgot where they were going. And they forgot who you were. But you fought the tricks of the mist, and your mind remained clear. You tried to explain to them. You wanted them to listen. But they blamed

you instead. They saw their misery written on your hands. They gave you their shortcomings, and in the end it was too heavy, too much—you grew tired under the weight, and in your weakness they were able to lift you and toss you overboard, but your hair—your beautiful, beautiful hair, that your mother brushed for you before she died—caught on the boat and you refused to sink. So they cut it. One lock, one slice, that's all it took for you to slip away.

There is no pain where you are now. There are other things. Timelessness. The everlasting smell of orchids. Isa. Birdsong. You move among all of it, unseen, but felt. Cherished. You have developed a keen sense of the living—not what they show, but who they are. You can see inside their souls, and you are often left wanting.

You have learned that patience is a gift.

You have learned that perseverance is a necessity.

You have learned that creatures can be cruel, but many can be kind.

You have learned to ignore the call of the whenbo.

You have learned that compassion is life's greatest virtue.

You have learned of a girl who believed in you.

I know it's not you who dried the earth, you heard the girl say.

If I had known you then, we would have been friends.

That same girl made you a promise.

If I find your hair, I will cherish it.

Though your hair will never be found, it is a beautiful promise.

When you saw this girl set forth into the sea, just as you had, you wanted to learn other things.

You wondered: What if I whispered into the ear of a pahaalusk?

Animals, trees, earth—they understand things that other creatures do not.

So you leaned close to the pahaalusk's ear, and you told the girl's story. When you were finished, the pahaalusk set its eyes onto the sea and went into the water, toward the girl, and you were delighted.

And here is something else you learned:

How to pick osabana.

How to move about with fruit in the land of the living.

How to place it at someone's feet.

And you consider this your greatest achievement of all.

Fei Diwata

Lalani planned to run.

She would run as fast as she could.

She would run as far as her legs would take her.

She would climb the mountain, stand triumphantly on its summit, and humble herself before Fei Diwata.

She thought of her mother and the bloody cloth. Toppi's wails. Veyda and her empty basket. My-Shek. She thought of Usoa, dying alone in the belly of a tree.

All of this would move her forward, step by step, until she reached the top.

* * *

That's not what happened.

When Lalani ran past Bai-Vinca's body, she forgot to avoid the mounds.

The nunso shot out of the earth with no warning and grabbed hold of Lalani's ankles. She saw no face, no body, no head. Only dry and callused fingers. Nails that scratched her skin. Pale flesh dotted with white hair that made her think of Ellseth. The nunso tugged and pulled, and when Lalani fell, her chin hit the ground and her teeth hit her tongue and her mouth pooled with blood. She reached out, buried her fingers in the dirt, and pulled, pulled, pulled, desperate to escape the nunso's grip, but it was strong, and soon there were multiple hands holding her, and how was she to defeat them? She scraped and spit and howled, but she was losing.

She reached for the pouch.

Got the arrowhead.

Dropped it.

Spit.

She was buried to the knee and bent at an awkward

angle as her hand scrambled, searching for the arrowhead. But each time she thought her fingertip brushed its serrated edge, she lost it again.

She had no other weapons.

Scream.

That's all she had left.

And that's what she did.

She screamed.

She screamed "*No*" and "*Let me go*" and "*Stop*" and "*You won't get me*" and "*I'm stronger than you*" and even if she didn't know if she was telling the truth or not, she didn't care, she screamed it anyway, she would say it and make it true just as Lo Yuzi had taught her, and she did it again and again and blood dripped down her throat and made her cough, and still she kept screaming, even though her head hurt now more than ever.

At what point did the nunso let her go?

She didn't know. After she'd rested long enough to take a breath or two, she found the arrowhead and put it back in its pouch. She was free.

One fat, bloody lip.

One sliced cheek.

One sliced ear.

One empty stomach.

One swollen arm.

Feet caked in dirt, with scrapes and cuts from the forest floor.

A bloodied leg where the nunso's fingernails had raked her skin.

Head, sore and aching.

Parched throat.

Weary lungs.

Two bloody hands.

Nevertheless, she walked.

Carefully. Slowly. Her body was hungry and exhausted, and eventually she could no longer walk properly. Not to mention that terrible, terrible ache in her eyes and the strange visions in her head—images of Veyda and Hetsbi and Drum and her mother that didn't make any sense. At times she felt as she had in the scouting boat. Confused. Unsure of who she was or what she was doing.

Then the sun set.

The darkness made it even more difficult to keep going, especially since she was hungry and thirsty.

That's when she fell.

She collapsed, like a leaf drifting from a tree. Her fall was quiet, and once she was down, she stayed there. She woke up one time, to eat osabana from the pyramid of fruit that appeared before her, within arm's reach. She didn't even have to sit up. She bit into it, peel and everything, and chewed. The osabana burned her lip, but so what? It's amazing the things that no longer matter when you are hungry enough.

The second time she fell, it was at the base of Mount Isa.

She'd found her way to open land. The horizon was flat. She'd expected a cluster of trees or peaks, but that didn't matter because in the distance, rising like a perfect, round sun, was the mountain.

By now, she knew she was ill.

She knew she was very ill indeed.

A fever ran through her body; it made her sweat. She was hot and cold all at once. The nausea was relentless. But she managed to pick up her pace with the mountain in sight. She moved briskly, holding her belly, lifting her shoulder to wipe blood from her cheek, wincing. She walked like this for a mile or so, and then she was at the foot of the mountain.

Except.

There was no mountain.

The horizon had played tricks on her.

There was only a hill.

A single hill with a tree on top.

She made a small, quiet sound, like a whimper.

She fell again.

Lalani thought that was the end of her story. She thought she was a girl who had gone on a journey, suffered many hardships, and would now drift away, having accomplished nothing.

So after she fell the last time, she stayed there. She inhaled the smell of fragrant grass. She felt the blades against her cheek. She closed her eyes.

When did she open them again?

When she heard a sound. Getting closer.

The pahaalusk. Its round, webbed feet pushing into the ground. Its soft eyes looking at her. It seemed to reach her quickly, though it moved slowly. The pahaalusk lowered its head and nudged its nose under Lalani's body. Was it nuzzling her? Perhaps it was afraid, too, but no—it was lifting her. It moved her onto its back, and now she was draped over its shell, holding on.

The pahaalusk moved gracefully for several hours. It placed her in front of a tree with a magnificent trunk. The bark coiled and twined into beautiful patterns all the way up, sprouting into heavy branches filled with hundreds of birds. There were so many that Lalani thought they were leaves at first.

It was such a wonderful sight that she forgot she was so miserable.

But only for a moment.

Lalani and the pahaalusk stared at the tree as the coils of the trunk moved and rearranged themselves. The trunk was thick and strong but seemed to move as easily as water. It was being pulled open, Lalani realized, by two brown hands emerging from the tree itself. A delicate foot followed. Then another.

A girl.

Her hair was bright and shining.

She wore a dress made of leaves and a belt of vine.

She was a small creature, even smaller than Lalani, but her eyes—brown and sparkling—held many secrets.

Something was slung across her back, but Lalani couldn't see what it was.

"Do you have my udyo?" the girl asked.

Her voice was delicate, too.

Lalani's mind tumbled. Udyo? She was so tired. Where had she heard that before?

She searched her memory and remembered Ellseth touching his magical cane to her knee.

"I'm Fei Diwata," the girl said. "Are you human? Why do you not stand? Do humans move about this way?"

I'm tired and ill, Lalani said. Or, she meant to say it.

Fei Diwata crouched in front of her, placed her hand on the pahaalusk's shell, and leaned forward. Her hair splayed across the ground like a dazzling puddle. Her lips were pink, and her breath smelled like flowers. She frowned and touched Lalani's cheek.

"You're hurt," Fei Diwata said.

Lalani found the strength to speak at last: "My friend, Usoa . . ."

"Ah, the mindoren."

"Yes."

"The nunso are taking care of her. She will be fine."

"The nunso? But I thought . . ."

"They are complicated creatures. But aren't we all?"

Lalani tasted dirt on her tongue, and blood.

"You've been bitten by a goyuk," Fei Diwata said. "You need to eat one of my osnoom."

"Osnoom?"

Fei Diwata disappeared. When she reappeared, she was holding a flower. Bright yellow, with specks of white.

"Here." Fei Diwata plucked off a petal and placed it in Lalani's mouth. "Don't worry, I have gardens full of them."

The osnoom tasted sweet and bitter all at once. Before Lalani could decide whether to chew or swallow it whole, the petal melted onto her tongue and Fei Diwata replaced it with another one.

Lalani wondered how many bushels of osnoom she could carry back to Sanlagita. Would Fei Diwata be willing to part with any seeds? Ditasa-Ulod had made it sound as if Fei Diwata would never help a human.

What had Ditasa-Ulod said?

Fei Diwata sees into the hearts of all living things. And she prizes one virtue above all else. If she looks into your heart and doesn't see it there, you will die. Do you want to die?

"I don't want to die," Lalani muttered.

"You won't die if you eat my osnoom," Fei Diwata said. After she placed the third petal on Lalani's tongue, she asked, "Have you seen my udyo?"

The udyo?

She was asking about Ellseth's cane, wasn't she?

"Your udyo was lost," Lalani said. She groaned. She ached so badly. "It was lost when our mountain broke open. I'm sorry." She spit blood into the dirt.

Fei Diwata puckered her lips. "That's strange, because I sense that it is very near," she said. She cast her eyes at the pahaalusk and studied him from under her dark lashes. "Perhaps this creature has it."

"I saw it disappear," Lalani said.

"What's that around your neck?"

"It's a pouch I took from a mindoren before he died. I didn't mean to steal it. I was trying to save him, but . . ." Lalani replied. "His name was Ellseth."

"Ellseth is the mindoren who stole my udyo," Fei Diwata said. She took the pouch from Lalani's neck and worked it open with her small fingers. When the arrowhead fell into her palm, her mouth curved into a perfect O. "This is it! You *do* have it!"

"No," Lalani said. "This is just an arrowhead."

Fei Diwata raised an eyebrow. "I know my own udyo."

She reached behind her and grasped the strange object slung across her back.

"This is my bow and arrow," Fei Diwata said proudly. She kissed the arrowhead and shoved it in place. "See? My udyo."

"But how—" Lalani began.

How could such a small thing make such a big difference?

Fei Diwata strode forward, closing the distance between herself and her tree. She aimed her arrow. It sailed through the air and landed in the trunk between two coils in the bark. The tree immediately sprang to life. All those birds—hundreds of them, impossible to count—spread their wings and took flight. There was a sound unlike anything Lalani had ever heard. A most beautiful music.

"Birdsong . . ." Fei Diwata said, "carries all of life's good fortunes."

Rise

Drum and Kul left after first dawn several days later. Did they believe they would make it? No one could tell. Their faces were hard as stone and never wavered—not as they boarded the ship, not as they gave their speeches, not as the ship pushed away from Sanlagita with a thick crowd of villagers looking on.

No one cheered.

Veyda, Cade, Hetsbi, and Lo Yuzi watched silently, elbow to elbow.

The water lapped against the sides of the boat.

They heard every splash. They heard their beating hearts. They felt a breeze from the distant sea.

Veyda and Hetsbi started a new routine. They met Cade in the dark and the three of them walked to the northern shore together, Veyda following Cade, Hetsbi behind her. They sat together, watching and waiting.

Night after night.

"What if Drum and Kul make it across the sea and Lalani is there, too? What if they find her?" Hetsbi asked one night, his voice like a cresting wave.

They had discussed this before, of course.

But surely Drum and Kul wouldn't make it—would they?

No, they would not.

The ship appeared on the fifth daybreak, but it didn't announce itself from the fog intact. It arrived on the waves in pieces. One board, followed by another. Ragged and splintered. Perhaps the ship had fallen apart in a storm. Perhaps something had taken a bite out of it.

As pieces of wood wandered to shore, Veyda, Hetsbi, and Cade gathered them and wondered: What if Drum and Kul had still survived, somehow?

Their answer came soon enough.

Drifting in with the tide: a man's arm, cut off at the elbow, clutching a gavel. Veyda was the first to see it, and she didn't waste a moment. She grabbed the gavel and ran to the village. Her hair trailed in the wind behind her. Her feet pounded the earth. The gavel was heavy, but weightless.

When she arrived at the gong, she stopped. A cloud of dust puffed around her.

She heaved her arms back and swung. The sound vibrated through her wrist, into her elbow, and across her shoulders to her heart. She hit the gong again and again, until she couldn't do it any longer. Then she dropped the gavel to the ground and waited for the villagers.

But she heard something else instead.

Strange. Miraculous.

She lifted her chin to find out where the sound was coming from and squinted into the sky, which had suddenly brightened. Music—yes, it was *music*. She had never heard anything like it before.

Birds.

Birds—hundreds of them.

But not all of them were singing. Some carried plants in their beaks. Plants with thorny stems. Plants with leaves and berries. Plants heavy with possibility. And they carried flowers, too. Yellow flowers speckled with white. And Veyda watched, wide-eyed and curious, as plants, flowers, and seeds rained down around her, one by one.

Pointed to the Sea

When Veyda ran off, Cade was at her heels. He was there to hear the gong. He saw the first flight of birds, just like she did. But not Hetsbi. He had been ready to follow—he had his feet pointed in that direction, even—but something stopped him. A break in the mist.

His heart thundered. What if it was Kul, clutching desperately on a piece of driftwood? And here he was, alone. He squinted his eyes for a better look. A long gaze over his shoulder.

No, it wasn't a piece of driftwood.

It was a ship.

No, not a ship. A boat.

His boat.

He would have recognized it anywhere, even from a hundred miles away. It was the boat that would never sail, the one left for scrap.

But it didn't make any sense. His boat had been discarded with the others. Destined for nothing.

He turned around. How had his boat managed to crawl across the shore and drift into the current by itself? But now he saw that was not what had happened at all. There was someone *inside* the boat. A small outline that came into focus as the fog slipped away. Here was the dark hair. Here were the wide-set eyes. Here was the round face.

"Lalani," he said.

You Are a Sanlagitan

Imagine you're a Sanlagitan. Things are no longer as they were. You don't know everything about how a twelve-year-old girl made it to Isa and back again. Nevertheless, she is here. She arrived one morning like a ghost. No, not a ghost. She was an ordinary girl, made of flesh and blood. She arrived when the morning sun was just hitting the water. She was paddling a small scouting boat with a pahaalusk at her side. There was a tower of orange fruit in the bow.

Look at the pitched roofs of the flenka houses, covered with thick meha leaves. There is the water well, in the center of the village, and a bright garden blooming with yellow flowers. And here is the schoolhouse, where boys learn to become men, and Veyda Yuzi teaches girls—and some boys, such as her brother—how to turn plants into medicine. There are plenty of plants for this purpose. The island is lush with them.

There is birdsong. There is more than enough. You see Lalani and her mother, walking along the shore, carrying their fishing nets. They have a pen of shek who are never thirsty. They weave soft wool and dye it in the brightest colors, shades that Sanlagitans had never seen, like purple and marigold.

The Sailing Days are no more. For now, there is no need. It is best to leave Isa to Isa. The village celebrates something else instead—the day a girl climbed out of an abandoned scouting boat and came back home.

Lalani Sarita.

Lalani of the distant sea.

ALSO BY ERIN ENTRADA KELLY

HELLO, UNIVERSE

Some friendships are meant to be

ERIN ENTRADA KELLY
Winner of the Newbery Medal

TURN THE PAGE TO READ AN EXTRACT . . .

Piccadilly
PRESS

1
Grand Failure

Eleven-year-old Virgil Salinas already regretted the rest of middle school, and he'd only just finished sixth grade. He imagined all those years stretching ahead of him like a long line of hurdles, each of them getting taller, thicker, and heavier, and him standing in front of them on his weak and skinny legs. He was no good at hurdles. He'd found this out the hard way: in gym class, where he was the smallest, most forgettable, and always picked last.

All things considered, he should have been happy on the last day of school. The year was over. He should have been skipping home, ready to tackle the bright summer ahead. Instead he walked through the front door like a defeated athlete—head low, shoulders hunched, a sack of disappointment sitting on his chest like an anvil. Because today, it was official: he was a Grand Failure.

"Oy, Virgilio," said his grandmother—his Lola—when he came in. She didn't look up. She was in the kitchen, slicing a mango. "Come take one of these. Your mother bought too many again. They were on sale, so she buys ten. And what do we need ten mangoes for? They're not even from the Philippines. They're from Venezuela. Your mother bought ten Venezuelan mangoes, and for what? That woman would buy kisses from Judas if they were on sale."

She shook her head.

Virgil straightened his posture so Lola wouldn't

suspect anything was wrong. He took a mango from the fruit bowl. Lola's eyebrows immediately scrunched together. Only they weren't really eyebrows, because she'd plucked them clean.

"What's wrong? Why you have that look?" she said.

"What look?" Virgil said.

"You know." Lola didn't like to explain herself. "Is that pug-faced boy at school being mean to you again?"

"No, Lola." For once, that was the least of his worries. "Everything's fine."

"Hmm," said Lola. She knew everything wasn't fine. She noticed everything about him. They had a secret kinship. It'd been that way ever since the first day she'd come from the Philippines to live with them. On the morning she arrived, Virgil's parents and identical twin brothers immediately rushed her in a flood of hugs and hellos. With the exception of Virgil, that's how the Salinas family was—big personalities that bubbled over like pots of soup. Virgil felt like unbuttered toast standing next to them.

"*Ay sus*, my first moments in America will be filled with a pulsing headache," Lola said. She pressed her fingertips to her temples and waved toward Virgil's older brothers, who were tall and lean and muscled, even then. "Joselito, Julius, fetch my bags, hah? I want to say hello to my youngest grandson."

After Joselito and Julius scurried off—ever the helpful brothers—Virgil's parents presented him like a rare exhibit they didn't quite understand.

"This is Turtle," his mother said.

That was their name for him: Turtle. Because he wouldn't "come out of his shell." Every time they said it, a piece of him broke.

Lola had squatted in front of him and whispered, "You are my favorite, Virgilio." Then she put her fingers to her lips and said, "Don't tell your brothers."

That was six years ago, and he knew he was still her favorite, even though she'd never said so again.

He could trust Lola. And maybe one day he would confess his secret to her, the one that made him a Grand Failure. But not now. Not today.

Lola took the mango from him.

"Let me slice that for you," she said.

Virgil stood next to her and watched. Lola was old and her fingers felt like paper, but she sliced mangoes like an artist. She started slowly, biding her time. "You know," she began, "I had a dream about the Stone Boy again last night."

She'd been dreaming about the Stone Boy for days now. The dream was always the same: a shy boy—not unlike Virgil—gets terribly lonely, takes a walk in the forest, and begs a rock to eat him. The biggest stone opens its gravelly mouth and the boy jumps inside, never to be seen again. When his parents find the stone, there is nothing they can do. Virgil wasn't sure how hard his parents would try to get him out anyway, but he knew Lola would hand chisel that rock to pieces if she had to.

"I promise not to jump into any rocks," Virgil said.

"I know there's something going on with you, *anak*. You have the face of Frederico the Sorrowful."

"Who is Frederico the Sorrowful?"

"He was a boy king who was sad all the time. But he didn't want anyone to know he was sad, because he wanted people to think he was a strong king. But one day he couldn't hold in his sorrows anymore. It all came out, just like a fountain." She lifted her hands in the air to mimic splashing water, still holding the paring knife in one of them. "He wept and wept until the whole land flooded and all the islands drifted away from each other. He wound up trapped on an island all alone until a crocodile came and ate him." She handed a beautiful slice of mango to Virgil. "Here."

Virgil took it. "Lola, can I ask you a question?"

"If you ever have a question, ask it."

"How come so many of your stories have boys getting eaten by stuff, like rocks or crocodiles?"

"Not all of them are about boys getting eaten. Sometimes it's girls." Lola tossed the knife into the sink and raised her non-eyebrows. "If you decide to talk, you come find your Lola. Don't burst like a fountain and float away."

"Okay," Virgil said. "I'm going to my room to check on Gulliver, make sure he's okay."

Gulliver, his pet guinea pig, was always happy to see him. He would chirp as soon as Virgil opened the door; he knew it. Maybe he wouldn't feel like such a failure then.

"Why wouldn't he be okay?" Lola called out as Virgil walked toward his room. "Guinea pigs can't get in much trouble, *anak*."

Virgil could hear her laughing as he placed the mango between his teeth.

2
Valencia

I'm not sure what God looks like. I don't know if there's one big God in heaven or if there's two or three or thirty, or maybe one for each person. I'm not sure if God is a boy or a girl or an old man with a white beard. But it doesn't matter. I just feel safe knowing someone's listening.

I mostly talk to Saint Rene. His real name is Renatus Goupil. He was a French missionary who traveled to Canada. While he was there, he made the sign of the cross over a kid's head and they thought he was spreading curses, so they took him prisoner and killed him.

I found out about him because on my tenth birthday, this girl Roberta gave me a book called *Famous Deaf People in History*. I would have never given Roberta a book about *Famous Blond People* or *Famous People Who Talk Too Much* or *Famous People Who Tried to Cheat Off My Spelling Paper*—all of which describe Roberta—but the good thing was that I found out about Saint Rene.

I don't know sign language but I taught myself the alphabet so I made up a sign name for Saint Rene. I cross my middle finger over my index finger—the sign for R—and tap it three times lightly against my lips. That's one of the first things I do after I take off my hearing aids for the night. Then I stare at the ceiling and imagine my prayers traveling up, up, up and hovering over my bed until they lift all the way through the roof. Then I imagine them landing on a cloud and sitting there, waiting to be answered.

When I was younger, I thought the cloud would get so heavy that all my prayers would come falling down and I'd have everything I wished for, but now I'm eleven so I know better. I still picture them sailing up, though. There's no harm in that.

I only pray at night, because it's my least favorite time of day. Everything is still and dark, and I have too much time to think. One thought leads to another until it's two in the morning and I haven't slept a wink. Or I've slept, but not well.

I didn't always hate the nighttime.

I used to crawl into bed and drift off to sleep, no problem.

It's not because of the dark. That's never bothered me. One time my parents took me to this place called Crystal Caverns where you went underground and couldn't even see your hand in front of your face. I wasn't scared at all. I loved it down there. I felt like an explorer. Afterward my dad bought me a souvenir snow globe, only there are bats inside instead of snow. I keep it right next to me, on my nightstand, and I shake it before I go to sleep, just because.

So it's not the dark that keeps me awake.

It's the nightmare.

The nightmare goes like this.

I'm standing in a big open field—one I've never stood in before. The grass is yellow and brown under my feet, and I'm surrounded by thick crowds of people. Nightmare Me knows who they are, even though they don't look like anyone I know in real life. They all look at me with round black eyes. Eyes without whites in them. Then a girl in a blue dress steps forward, away from the crowd. She says two words: "solar eclipse." I know what she's saying even though I'm not wearing my hearing aids and she doesn't move her mouth. That's how it is in dreams sometimes.

The girl is pointing skyward.

Nightmare Me looks up to where she's pointing and watches attentively, not scared yet. I crane my neck, along with everyone else. We all watch as the moon moves in front of the sun. The blazing blue sky turns gray, then dark, and Nightmare Me thinks it's the most amazing thing I've ever seen.

It's strange how nightmares work, though.

Somehow Nightmare Me knows things won't end well. As soon as the moon finishes passing the sun, my blood rushes into my ears and my palms dampen with sweat. I look down from the sky—slowly, slowly, not wanting to see—and just as I suspected, everyone is gone. The whole crowd. Even the girl in the dress. Nothing moves. Not one single blade of grass. The field stretches on for miles and miles. The moon has pulled everyone away. All but Nightmare Me.

I'm the only person on the face of the earth.